THE RAT CATCHER

Author: Max Manus

Copyright: George Manus

Design and Layout: Ole Praud

Publisher: BoD • Books on Demand GmbH, In de Tarpen 42, 22848 Norderstedt, Germany

Print: Libri Plureos GmbH, Friedensallee 273, 22763 Hamburg, Germany

George's online bookstore -
www.georgemanus-books.com

The Art of George Manus online store -
www.georgemanus.com

George's innovation & hub website -
www.maxmanusinnovation.com

George Manus - mail:
info@georgemanus.com

ISBN: 978-87-4305-824-3

Books written by Max Manus:

Det vil helst gå godt, 1945

Det blir alvor, 1946

Underwater Saboteur (1953 by William Kimber & Co. Ltd., and in 1972 by Fontana Books.)

Jorden rundt på 80 dager, 1973, (with Arne Falk-Rønne).

Reisen til verdens ende, 1975, (with Arne Falk-Rønne).

Sally Olsen: Fangenes engel i Puerto Rico, 1975.

Rottejegeren: Written by Max in 1948 - published by Kagge Forlag AS (Oslo) in 2021.

Introduction

George Manus

Rat Catcher was the name given to the Norwegian resistance fighters who carried out the dirtiest jobs during the second world war. They exterminated or, liquidated, informers, torturers and other Norwegians who worked for the Germans.

The post-war period of war history is fascinating yet has been mostly concealed. In this short novel written in 1948 by my stepfather Max Manus, a well-known resistance fighter, it tells a story of the *Rat Catchers*. At the centre is Max's alter ego Freddy and a group of veterans. They try to find love and their place in society but drown out the bad memories from the days of war in different ways.

We actually know quite a lot about my stepfather Max Manus - as early as 1945 he published *Det vil helst gå godt*, followed by *Det blir alvor in* 1946, and in 1995 *Mitt liv (My Life)* was published. In addition, the book *Tikken*, which is about my mother, was published in 2009.

Max's war books were a success. He himself claimed that only the Bible sold more in the post-war years!

People were keen to know what kind of life the boys really lived during the war. In 2008 the film Max Manus became a blockbuster and the most watched movie in Norway. It was directed by Joachim and Espen Sandberg (Pirates of Caribbean, Maleficent: Mistress of Evil, Kon-Tiki,

Bandidas).

It shows authentically, as my mother confirmed, what the atmosphere was like during the war, and what role Max had played.

The story told in **The Rat Catcher** (**Rottejegeren** in Norwegian) is from the years immediately after the war, and we assume that Max wrote it in 1948. After all he felt he had proven to himself and the world that he could write.

His joint company *Clausen & Manus* did not demand too much from him so in 1953 he started his own company, *Max Manus Kontormaskiner* (supplier of office machines).

The Rat Catcher was written on a travel typewriter. Every millimetre of the A4 sheet was utilised, with compact text, without line breaks, and with infinitely long sentences and commas in the strangest of places. The language was a mixture of Danish and Norwegian with spelling mistakes all over, however, what Max lacked in correct Norwegian, he made up for in his story telling.

The family has no idea why the script was never published. Nor why mother, who was Max's secretary, did not rewrite the manuscript. We all knew that the script existed, and that it was kept in a yellow folder in the bottom drawer of the rose-painted cupboard, at our home on Landøya in Asker, outside Oslo.

My mother gave me the manuscript of **The Rat**

Catcher as a gift. It was not the original, but a copy. The original, my brother says, was bound by him at Blinderen University in 1976, at the same time as his main thesis, and was given to Max as a gift for his sixtieth birthday. To this day no one knows where the bound script is.

In the spring of 2020 I was 81 and had in previous years spent a lot of time with my own writings. In other words I already had some insight into what it means to publish one's own books. With new enthusiasm, action was taken by my sister Mette to explore the possibilities of publishing it.

The book could certainly, in the hands of qualified people, become the basis for further elaboration of the theme and thereby perhaps historically become more interesting, but together with the publisher Kagge Forlag the decision was taken to print it just as Max wrote it, with only some small judicious edits which I am responsible for.

After it became a best-seller in Norway in 2021, I took it upon myself to translate it into English, being very careful not to alter the original novel. It has then been proof read by my friend and native Englishman Spencer Smith (Yin Yang Studios).

To me *The Rat Catcher* is a wonderful insight into human reactions and feelings of people in what was a unique time of liberation after the second world war. For further insight and a taste of more writings from my step father I include at the end of the book two excerpts from his book *Underwater Saboteur.*

There is speculation surrounding whether Max at some point, was himself an active *Rat Catcher.* The family refrain from taking a fixed opinion on this, but we all remember that mother, when asked directly, distanced herself from him being a *Rat Catcher.*

George Manus
Autumn 2023

var de blitt,litt triste,litt trette,og de levet opp igjenn det som engang var,en selde
merkelig tid. London i krigstid.De levet opp igjenn stemningen fra mangen enn natt med
søte små engelske piker,rikelig med penger,hyggelige mennesker,og godt kammeratskap.
De kunne se for seg ~~Piccadilly~~ det mørklagte Picadilly,med syngende og elskende menneske
i mørket.Overalt uniformer,og alle som hadde uniformer var like.Den engelske flykaptein
som kanskje var adelig.Den polske greve.Den danske sjømann,og den norske visergutt.Kans
de den natten mens luftforsvaret skjøt som hårdest på de tyske fly,og bombene haglet
over London fandt hverandre og blev som en stor familie,på tross av at de knapt forstod
hverandre.Kanskje visergutten,og skolegutten fra Oslo fandt dem selv blandt tyve andre
hjemme hos en ung dame ut på natten,i ett hus som de hidtil bare hadde lest om.Og var
visergutten kanskje bitter mot de rike i samfundet,fandt han her ut at i krig når det
gjelder"to be or not to be " er det mannen det kommer ann på,og ikke hvad hans far er.
Nu satt de her og sang,og prøvet å leve det alt om igjenn,men den tid vil aldri komme
tilbake.De venner vi fikk under krigen er glidd ut av bildet,de passet ikke i fredstid
eller vi passet kanskje ikke dem.Vårt very charming englich er blit dårligt engelsk,
og da den smarte uniformen forsvant kom konfeksjonsdressen frem.Enda verre var det for d
guttene som giftet seg og i troen på det Norge som skulle reise seg bare vi ble frie,
fyldte sine små engelske misser med historier som tydet på at de var norske adelsmenn
hviss godser ikke lå tilbake for de engelske.Det var ikke deres skyld at fantasien spil
let dem et lite puss,når de stadig ventet på å bli drept.Og det var ikke deres skyld
at forholdene blev slik efter krigen,at det å ha vært i England og kjempet for Norge
nesten var blitt en skam,det var i allefald det inntrykk mann fikk på boligkontorene.
Freddy satt og døset og filosoferte,pokkeren nu er flasken tom sa Knut.-Well så var
der ikke annet å gjøre enn å gå hjem.Da de stod utenfor på gaten så de at himlen var
klarnet,som på komando begynte alle tre og slå lens,mens de stirte opp på himlen.
Ingen sa noe,der var døds stille i byen.Skvalpingen fra pisset lød kraftigt i natten.
"Aksjon station " sa plutselig Harald. Freddy hadde nettopp stått og tenkt på det samme
Ja er det ikke rart sa knut,hvergang jeg ser på himlen om natten,tenker jeg på fledskje
hoppingen,jeg er så gla at jeg slipper det igjen." Å vi må nokk til om ikke så lenge
igjenn sa Harald " Det er snart samme faen hvad som skjer sa Freddy,men jeg er nu glad
over at jeg ikke sitter derinne,sa han og pekte med hodet over mot den dystre konturen
av møllergt.19. " Ja meg skal de aldri få levende innenfor igjenn sa Knut innbitt "
Men hvilken vei skal Dere,jeg skal bortover torvgaten,jeg har en jente jeg kan ligge
hos i natt.Da de andre skulle mot vestkanten skiltes de med et koselig kvell,og
so long. Freddy ville gjerne bli alene nu så han sa at han skulle en annen vei enn han
igrunnen skulle.Harald trykket ham veldigt i hånden og takket for at så hyggeligt hadd
han ikke hatt det på lenge,og nu måtte de sees oftere.Freddy var glad da han så Harald
stime bortover gaten forbi justisbygningen oppover mot vergelandsveien.
Freddy slentret bortover mot Stortorvet,han kjente at han var trett,men alikevell var
der kommet en slik uro i ham,at han viste at det ville bli vanskeligt å få sove.
På stortorvet gikk han inn i en telefonboks,han la ti øre på telefonen.summetonen kom
men så angret han seg.Han trykket på knappen og fikk tiøren tilbake.Det ville være
å ringe til henne så sent på kvelden,han fikk heller ta til sin kone.
Han gikk bortover gaten,men så bråsnudde han og gikk tilbake til telefonboksen,han la
tiøren igjenn,og ventet på summetonen,og så slog han ett nummer på telefonen.Han kunne
høre telefonen ringte,og han lurte på hvad som nu ville skje.Plutselig slog en tanke ned
ham,Tenk om hun hadde en mann hos seg.Han ville legge på røret igjenn,men så hørte han he
nes stemme på den andre siden av tråden.En søvnig men klar stemme som sa Hallo-
Freddy ville si noe men det blev bare ett grøtet grynt,han kremtet,og la hatten ved side
av telefonen.Er det deg Gerd,sa han så.Ja svarte stemmen. Det er Freddy. Han hørte at de
søvnige forsvant fra stemmen,og den hørtes opphisset ut da hun spurgte om der var noe ga
Nei sa Freddy,men jeg er litt ute av ikke vekt,jeg har lyst til å gå hjem i natt,kan
du ikke rive i en kopp kaffe på meg.Stemmen ~~bixxxxitxxxlig~~ på den andre siden blev hel
rolig og ~~kxit~~ behersket. Bare kom med engang så skal jeg møte deg i porten.det er ikke
gtb du vekker opp hele huset.Hvor er du henne..Freddy sa at han var på Storto
vet men der var ingen drosjer så holdeplassen så han ville bruke en 15 minutter på å gå
opp til der hun bodde i Parkveien..O.K. sa stemmen i telefonen,jeg setter på kaffen nu.
Freddy hang opp telefonen,tok sin hatt og gikk ut av boksen.En drosjebil stoppet i gaten
snudde og kjørte opp på holdeplassen.Freddy langet ut oppover grensen. Han så på klokke
sin,han ville være der presis om 15 minnutter. Tankene begynte å kretse om det som kunne
~~c~~kje.Men så prøvet han å tvinge tankerne inn i en annen retning.Han tenkte på Gerd slik
som hun var under krigen,og hvad hun hadde betydd for ham i hans arbeide.Han prøvet å se
henne for seg som den gode og reelle kammerat som hadde delt godt og ondt sammen med gut
,og litt efter litt gled den erotiske villskapen som var flammet opp i ham ved tanken
på at han skulle til henne på denne tid av natten,og ved hennes ord om at hun møtte ham
i porten for at ingen skulle bli vekket,vekk,og kammeratskapsføelsen tok overhånd.
En bil gled plutselig lydløst opp ved siden av Freddy,og Freddy skvatt voldsomt og hans
hånd gikk automatisk inn i armhulen og grep om pistolen,så han at det var Politiets
~~natruljevogn.~~Bilen stoppet og de to politibetjentene som satt forann ble sittende og sti

*Max with his portable typewriter on which he
wrote **The Rat Catcher** in 1948*

CHAPTER 1

The rain splashes *down*, and the same strange old feeling explodes in his chest. The memories come and go as he trudges along the streets in the dark autumn night. In a particularly dark place in the street, he stops for a moment, and as he pretends to pull his raincoat tighter around his neck, he takes a good look around.

Not spotting any people, he slips his hand under his armpit. He moves the gun from his armpit into his coat pocket. It's nice to feel the wonderful sense of security that the touch of a gun always gave him. His cigarette has gone out a long time ago, he puts the rain soaked stub in his mouth, however reluctantly he wants to - he has to spit out the remains.

He dreams more and more back to the time when it was serious. The time when he had a task, and life really seemed to have meaning. How far it was - and yet so damned close. Tonight he feels more intensely than ever how lonely he is, and how foolish his whole life seems to him. This life which for five long years he has fought so hard to preserve.

His innate sense of humour is slowly starting to help him get back on track. Although it's a chore, he stops and unbuttons his coat so he can reach into his trouser pocket for his cigarettes and matches. With his cigarette lit again, he felt significantly better and saw the situation a little brighter.

Freddy, he says to himself, *you are a fool. Come down to earth. You have never had as good a time in your life as you have now.*

He then tries to hum a little to himself and involuntarily begins to go to a beat, then the hum takes the form of a march. The lyrics are English and it seems that the melody fits particularly well tonight.

'She'll be coming round the mountain when she comes'.

Gods know how many times he marched to it in Scotland during the war. And now the memories come back. It's no use trying to forget. Will he ever forget? Will anybody in this strange little country of ours forget?

Sometimes he has the feeling that people would only look back - and not forward. How ridiculous all these fools are who will tell all men to their uttermost in life and death, how heroic they had behaved in such and such a situation. It is almost as if their life depended on telling their story in such careful detail.

He has to smile when he thinks about his routine way of treating such heroes. Always the same interested expression and always the same remarks:

'Yes, I know you wouldn't have stood a chance if the Germans had found out.'

After all, it is the same boring insignificant stories about the man who had an underground resistance newspaper in his office or at home, and state police and Germans who for one reason or another had come near the place where the illegal newspaper was located.

Perhaps the person telling the story had worked for the Germans? And that this, with his efforts with the underground newspaper at the time when the Germans were actually not that far away - perhaps it had become his lifeline purely morally towards himself? It was perhaps supposed to cover his German work, which at the time he did not think or feel was so wrong, but which, after the war ended, he had perhaps begun to speculate a little about? There could be all kinds of motives.

Freddy never bothers to think about why he should be stuffed with these stories in life and death. But it is now always the same. Immediately a man realises that he is Freddy, and had been involved in sabotage, and that he must therefore have belonged to the sabotage company, then there is no way around it. He must - whether he wants to or not - listen to all the heroic stories. But there are also quite moving stories he gets to hear every now and then. About everyday life's real little heroes from those five long years.

Sometimes he can't stand the word resistance being mentioned. Still, he is like everyone else. Day after day, week after week, for over three long years, not a day had passed without him having spoken about the underground to someone. It was like a curse that followed him 24 hours a day, when he laid awake and in dreams when he slept. It toils and toils, steadily and surely on his nervous system. Every now and then he panics and then he waits for the bang, hoping only that they will miss or that the shot will not cripple him. It also happens that at times, when he sees life very bleakly, he actually waits for that liberating bullet to come.

But despite his melancholy and sometimes black outlook on life, he has an intense desire to live. Thank God this panic is becoming less and less frequent as time goes on. Sometimes he even goes to work without his gun on him. But he always puts his hand in his pocket when he enters the main entrance, or when he goes back through the gate.

He thinks of the old envy of the common man in the street. The envy which he suffered so greatly during the five years when he was constantly in fear of the day his luck would run out and was always prepared to die through the most sadistic torments that a human brain could devise.

And he does not forget the idiotic self-pity that he always suffered from, which at special moments can still bring tears to his eyes today. Or how he can also now stand and cry inside himself when he stands on a street corner waiting for something. Then it is just like he was waiting for the name that he had been ordered to delete from the list of informers, which had been sent from London.

Had the Nazis guessed what was stirring in him at such moments? Had they known how he had then envied the little clerk who might pass him in the street, half-starved, in only the most necessary rags, when, due to the lack of food and the unwillingness not to profit from the misfortune of his fellow man, he had to sell everything of value to buy food?

First various objects in the home, then clothes. He was not well, the little common man in the street.

After all, he didn't risk having to do such work.

It was now also hell that he was going to become a specialist, what they in London called a *Rat Catcher*. To this day, so many years later, he still has to struggle with this cursed *Rat Catching*. Drunk or sober. Night or day. The memories never leave him. Once, when he was slightly drunk, his self-pity and inebriation brought him to tears and he told one of the boys that the only moment he had peace from *Rat Catching* was when he was sleeping with his wife.

For good reasons therefore, the peace he then gets in his soul cannot last more than a few moments compared to the long hours that 24 hours of sleeplessness can bring out of an ordinary day.

In itself, there was never any reason for him to regret the *Rat Catching*. He had saved the state a lot of trouble. Because when it really mattered, he knew better than anyone what it meant to the Nazis when one of their most aggressive and dangerous men, despite the most incredible precautions, was gunned down, for example in the middle of the center of Oslo, with bodyguards in front and behind.

And there were certain cases which even today - so many years later - fill him with a certain perverse satisfaction. Like the time he emptied the entire magazine from a distance of two meters into the body of an informer who was also a sadistic torturer, and who he knew had been the worst of those who had tortured his younger childhood friend to death - a friend who was actually his only fixed point of contact in this life.

When he was asked if he wanted to take the job as a *Rat Catcher* his eyes had fallen on the name at the top of the list. He knew that this name covered the terrible beast in human form, which had cost the lives of so many Norwegian patriots. This name was probably the reason why he had taken on the job as a *Rat Catcher.*

This name would be removed from the list. It was thus his first so-called victim.

He thinks back to that morning when he stood in the hallway of the house on the west side, together with one of the boys, he can again sense the strange smell that was in the hallway.

His mate had said that Freddy had gone wild and used up the whole magazine. Well, they had gotten away, and well, there was some satisfaction in seeing the Nazis' fury at losing one of their best men.

But no, the *Rat Catching* itself didn't really bother him that much. It was all the good Norwegians who had been shot in retaliation that bothered him.

It was these memories that tormented him. He knew that sooner or later this was what would drive him mad.

He had done the most foolish things after liberation that no normal man would do. Things that indicated he had given in to an urge for perverted self-torture.

He had acquired another trauma to add to the many others, which he would never get rid of. He had gone up to Trandum where the German executioner, Oskar Hans, had shown where the bodies (of those whom the Germans had liquidated as revenge for the various victims of the **Rat Catchers**) were buried. It had been a perverse urge to torment himself when, after the terrible experience, he continued to go to all kinds of funerals where the weeping families paid their last respects to the victims of the Germans' reprisals.

The gods should know that after one of the Germans' high commanders had been shot and his entourage taken hostage, he had tried every opportunity to fall in battle.

But he is still alive. Now he has to pull himself together and let bygones be bygones.

CHAPTER 2

It stops raining. He suddenly gets an intense feeling of longing for his comrades from the time of the war. It's late, but maybe there is still someone over in the Club. It will be a long walk, but maybe he will get a taxi on the way.

Damn! No more cigarettes. Damn!

A car is coming. Freddy goes out into the street and waves and the car stops. It's a taxi.

Freddy gives the address of the Club to the driver as he turns around smiling and says:

'Oh! you are one of them? You're going to the X Club, aren't you?'

'Yes' replies Freddy and asks if the driver possibly has cigarettes. He gets one and the driver begins telling the story about what he, had done during the war.

Freddy leans back in the car's soft cushions and smokes his cigarette pleasantly. He hears the driver's voice; it is like a faint murmur.

The driver chats and chats and Freddy grunts once in a while to show his attention.

Suddenly he hears the driver say:

'I would probably have ended up on Victoria terrace

if he had realised that, but the Germans were so stupid.'

Yes, Freddy must agree. They were so stupid.

The taxi stops and Freddy gives a generous tip. The driver says it's fun to meet such a fellow and then drives off.

Freddy stays outside the Club for a while. It is right next to and overlooks one of the big prisons with iron bar and closed windows. Poor bastards sitting in there. Well, the times when the screams of the torturers echoed through the corridors are over. But that is also the end of the time when *"Ja, vi elsker"* (the Norwegian National Anthem) was sung from the cells. The atmosphere is altogether so completely different now.

During the war, a man could endure humiliation, torture and death. He could go to the judgment seat with his forehead raised. He could look his executioners in the eyes, and he could sing: *"Fight for everything you hold dear, die if it matters"*.

When the liberating shot came, the victim's last thought would be that there are others who continue, where I leave. We never give up!

The wretches who now take our places, the fellows who are now led to the judgment seat, are of a different cast. They know one thing: after us, no one will come. They are the last. That everything is hopelessly over. No one, when the death sentence is executed, will grit their teeth and say:

We never give up!

No mother would look demonstratively and reproachfully at her son, and demandingly point to the notice in the newspaper and say:

'Look what those pigs have done.'

We knew that every time one of us gave his life for the cause, hundreds of new ones entered, Freddy thinks.

There was increasingly strong opposition. We fought for what we loved, fought for our country, our people, our existence. But the others, what are they fighting for? They are now fighting for their lives, and when it's over, it's over.

The Club front door opens and a man comes out.

'Gee, is that you Freddy?'

I snapped: 'sure, I thought it was one of the runaways standing there to catch me.'

Freddy laughs.

'Yes, you had little chance. I would have shot you down before you had a chance to say *cake*.'

'Are you going home?'

'Yes, I have given it a thought.'

'Is there anyone in the Club?' Freddy asks.

'Yes, Knut and Harald are sitting in there and arguing as usual.'

The fellow, who had been standing in the door, followed Freddy inside. The Clubs premises were previously a small restaurant, and to be honest they were rather dark and sad. But if the premises were nothing special, the names in the guest book were so much more. Generally the Club had grown up under the strangest and most difficult conditions imaginable.

Freddy has to smile to himself when he thinks about the meetings he has attended. No matter what is proposed, there is always someone who objects. And when you do get to talk you are talked over. I guess it cannot be avoided when perhaps a hundred individuals have to make a joint decision.

He hears the voices of Knut and Harald. They are very excited. Knut is the one with the loudest voice so Freddy listens to him to try to understand what they are discussing.

That's the usual. Harald is hot-tempered and very interested in politics, and Knut loves to wind people up. Being interested in the military, Knut only needs to mention the Minister of Defence, and Harald explodes:

'I don't give a damn how he, the Minister of Defence, was during the war. It's just as well that if he has a job like this, and has been responsible for our entire defence, then it is not possible to only think about yourself and your own career.'

Freddy knows that here is a welcome opportunity to disconnect, and intervenes in the discussion by saying:

'I have understood it to mean that the Minister of Defence had taken up the position only after hard pressure, and very much against his will?'

Harald almost turns violet and explodes by saying that it is really strange that he is not more receptive to the pressure to make him withdraw from work.

'That way, our entire defence goes to hell!'

Now Knut gets the chance to say something. He hastens to say:

'The Minister of Defence is one of Norway's sharpest legal minds. The Prime Minister himself has said that it was a great asset for Norway to have such a force at the head of the defence. And if it was something that everyone had to know, it was that all the old officers were jealous of the new ones.'

'They had simply set up the campaign to overthrow the Minister of Defence.'

Harald understands that Knut wants him angry, so he controls himself and answers calmly:

'Even you, Knut, would not claim that any of the three generals who left in protest against the Minister of Defence could imagine the possibility of participating in a plot?'

Knut realises that the discussion is entering a more serious track and says to Freddy:

'Now you really have to take cover, Freddy! Those fellows who have escaped are not to be trifled with, and I think they have a bone to pick with you.'

Freddy laughs and throws his coat and hat over a chair. Then he remembers that he had taken the gun out of its holster and put it in his coat pocket. He takes it out of his pocket and slips it into place in his shoulder holster. Neither men makes any comment.

Knut asks if Freddy wants a small drink. 'Yes please', says Freddy and then asks what they're drinking.

'Aquavit and soda' answered Harald, still a little sullen.

'Toast!' Freddy says, taking a deep gulp. He leans back in his chair, letting the smoke rise as he looks around.

It's a shame that the venue is so unattractive. Various objects have been hung on the wall. A silk banner from the French resistance movement, souvenirs from the Danish resistance movement as well as greetings from the English, Americans, etc.

But there is also something else hanging there. Something that always makes Knut think, there are photographs hanging row after row. Photographs of handsome young boys. Fair, blue-eyed, dark - without exception with sparkling eyes. All possible types.

But what is common to all those hanging there on the wall is that they had given their lives for Norway's cause.

They had all believed that what they fought for was worth giving their lives for.

Freddy ponders, and suddenly he says out loud:

'I wonder if the guys', he nodded his head towards the pictures, 'would have died the way they did if they had assumed that today we are once again facing a new war.'

He points to one picture of a slim young boy with a KNS (Royal Norwegian sailing-club) hat and a blue sky as a background.

'I know that it was the belief that something good would come after this war, which enabled him to tie his shirt around his neck and tighten it, until the spark of life was extinguished.'

Neither Knut nor Harald say anything, and the fellow who had met Freddy at the door had left.

Freddy looks at Harald.

Harald is very young, only about 27-28 years old. A medium height, stout, square cut type with light curly hair and clear blue eyes. He had broken his nose once during a parachute jump over Norway. He had crushed it against the edge of the hole in the plane during the jump-out, and for good reasons there was no medical attention for a long time.

But Harald is not particularly worried about his nose.

Knut turns to Freddy:

'You, Freddy, do you think any of the Nazis ever think about liquidating us?'

Freddy thoughtfully takes a sip from his glass before answering, while he takes a quick glance towards Knut.

Knut is about Freddy's age, about 35 years old. Fairly thin and pale with little hair, almost black eyes, nervous movements. Always dark bags under the eyes and nicotine-stained fingers. Above average height and very shabby dressed.

Freddy pauses a little more before answering:

'Now that's difficult to answer. You know it doesn't take more than a single slightly confused Nazi soul to take you out. It could be a relative of one of those who was taken by us during the war, who thinks he has something to avenge.

But otherwise I don't believe it. And it is difficult. It would hit all Nazis in Norway very hard if something like this were to happen. Besides, it goes well with many of them. A whole bunch have been granted amnesty, and there are unlikely to be any more death sentences.'

'Geez, I'm so glad I didn't have such crappy work during the war, says Harald.'

Freddy sees that Knut is shaking. Freddy knows that at a very early stage Knut had been involved in a very traumatic event, where they had to liquidate a female informant.

CHAPTER 3

The gang had lured her into a trap by using her own terrible means: namely pretending that they could get her information that could lead to her seeing some Christmas presents at the expense of Norwegian patriots.

Once they had her trapped, they had driven her to a place of cover. There they had made her tell everything she knew. She had been much more dangerous than they had imagined. She did not hold back and explained in full detail the German's torture techniques. She had told how Norwegian patriots had broken down, and had not hidden the fact that she had taken part in the terrible interrogations which were based on sadistic torture, of both female and male Norwegian patriots.

When they had learned what they wanted, they had told her that she was now to be transported onward. She was brought down to the car and driven out to a deserted place near Oslo.

Here they had parked the car on a side road, and together with her had walked along the road to a bridge. Their plan was to shoot her, tie a huge stone to her corpse, and throw her into the deep river below the bridge.

The boys had been both excited and nervous at the thought of what was about to happen. From the moment they had trapped her, they had dreaded the step they would have to take. It was a terrible feeling to sit and talk to a woman and know that they would soon kill her. They had tried to tell themselves that she was a beast that needed to be exterminated, and were determined to complete the task.

The whole thing nearly went wrong when one of the guys suddenly lost control and hit the informer with his Totenschlæger (German baton). The end piece had fallen off, and he continued to strike and strike with only the spring. The girl screamed out, and Knut, who had been carrying up the heavy stone to attach to her, had to drop it and run to her.

The boy was now completely hysterical, the girl stood there with blood running down her face while trying to control herself and kept repeating:

'You'll have to excuse me for screaming, but he's hitting me.'

Knut ended it by putting a gun with a silencer to her temple and pulling the trigger. The girl had always been certain that she was going to be sent to Sweden, and had not understood that she was going to die until the bullet smashed its way through her brain.

Panic had now taken hold of the three men, they eased the body over the bridge railing into the river. Unfortunately the river was frozen so the body had been left on the ice and would be found as soon as it became daylight.

They also knew that Knut had thrown up afterwards, so it was no wonder that the boy was thin and pale and had blue rings under his eyes.

The worst thing is that to this day Knut seems to be completely out of balance. He is often quarrelsome, ill-tempered and drinks too much, at the same time no one is aware of what he does for a living. Knut is not very popular, but Freddy knows that deep down Knut is a good, wholesome guy when it comes down to it.

But the same thing might happen to himself. It is clear that Knut finds it even more difficult than Freddy to relax.

Freddy suddenly feels a strong warm, almost loving feeling rise up in him for Knut: poor damn thing, he feels like doing something for him.

'You, Knut, if you get something to drink and some food it will be on me. I have some money today, and you have contacts so you can manage it even if it's late at night.'

Knut walks over to the phone and a moment later he is talking to someone else.

Freddy takes out a hundred Norwegian Kroner. Knut throws on a raincoat and a shabby hat, and picks up a folder. Freddy gives him the hundred note and Knut disappears.

There is a bad atmosphere in the room. Freddy empties the bottle that is between his own glass and Harald's.

'Toast!' He says.

'Toast!' Replies Harald. 'You Freddy, do you think Knut is out of his mind? Didn't you have some knowledge of him during the war?'

There we have the old thing again, Freddy thinks. But out loud he says:

'Knut was fine during the war, and even though there is a bit of trouble with him now, Knut has become completely OK again.'

'Yes, you know that Knut loves to make me angry - but it is said that he is a communist?'

Freddy smiles a little:

'If Knut is a communist, then it is probably only to tease others.'

Harald is now very serious. He says:

'You see, Freddy, it's not much fun if we can't trust each other here in the Club. And you know you can't trust a communist. You can explain how much you want them to be good Norwegians, etc., but the fact is that if the communists themselves do not understand that they are a tool of Moscow, then the rest of us will have to pay for their stupidity. Besides, you probably know that not all communists are stupid. They have their leaders who are obviously in direct Russian service, and those fellows will probably know and exploit the entire communist flock.'

'I think that you are taking things a bit too hard

with regard to the communists', replies Freddy. 'We have easily been unfair to them. I mean our own domestic communists. The big guys abroad and the communists in Russia, you can't count on them. It is clear that they are like the devil on wheels, and that they want to subjugate the whole world is something everyone must understand.

'However, I believe that our own communists are so insignificant that they only play the role of extras in this big difficult game. It is conceivable that they would like to gain power one day, but I am sure that they will be horrified if the trolls ever spoke, and the Russians really marched into our country. It is easier to shout we demand! in Norwegian than in Russian.

'Actually, I don't think I should say that I am almost convinced - that most communists do not seriously dream of becoming traitors. But you are right that by then it is too late to regret. Then you know that we only have one thing to do, and that is to get back underground as quickly as possible.'

We hear a car brake outside and a door slam shut. It's Knut who has already returned with the food and liquor, and Freddy is trying to cheer him up.

'I wish we were back in Scotland now. I can feel my mouth watering at the thought of when we roasted the heart, kidneys and fillets from the freshly shot deer. Do you remember when we sat by the fireplace and roasted it on the spit?'

Harald jumps onto the chair and somersaults backwards. Then he creeps forward as if he had a rifle, suddenly he drops to the floor and eels into position. Then the imaginary rifle slowly comes into position.

'Bang!' he says, grinning as he tries to look angry.

Freddy smiles and shouts back. 'Did you get it?'

'Well, of course!' replies Harald. 'A huge buck.'

Knut has put down the package and is now smiling, almost mockingly, as he takes off his coat. Freddy knows that Knut had never been interested in hunting. Harald, who is a hunter in his own right, has become completely ecstatic.

'Damn it Freddy, we complained when we were in England, but yes, we had a good time! Just think of the time in Scotland. I can go completely wild thinking about the hunt over there. Do you remember the time we went game hunting? Especially the time when we were lying down watching the birds, and you didn't want us to shoot. God save me for a play. Since liberation, I have flown like a madman in the forest back home where I live, but I have hardly seen a feather.'

Freddy smiled at the thought. He was a born hunter and woodsman, and perhaps more than anyone else he appreciated the hunting and angling that was so wonderful in Scotland. He remembered well the night when Harald and he laid in the woods at *Forest Lodge* and heard and saw the whole wonderful spectacle of the *Capercaillies* courtship display.

At that time he had a lot of difficulties with his superiors and longed wildly to parachute into Norway.

He longed for the smell of the sun-warmed forest. He longed to draw into his lungs the purest and most wonderful air in the world - the forest air, mixed with the scent of pine needles that lay and were warmed in the spring sun. He longed to smell the freshly felled timber in the forests. The wonderful smell that was left when you dried your soaking wet, tar-smeared skis against a pile of timber, while you sat sunbathing, smoking a good pipe and having peace of mind and being able to forget war and hostility. Perhaps more than anyone else in Scotland he longed for home, but not like his comrades for a home, he had none, but for the great forests, for the wonderful life an outdoors man could have when he lived in Oslo.

He remembered why he had asked Harald not to shoot. It was impossible afterwards to explain to Harald what he had felt, but for some reason it was as if it were sacrilege to spoil the wonderful atmosphere that was in the forest that night. He had a vague notion that the *Capercaillies* who played, fought and showed off to the admiring hens were Norwegian - they were not Scottish. They had flown from Norway to Scotland, and they were refugees like himself. He felt the wildness of the *Capercaillies* spread to himself, an almost erotic excitement when one of the hens coquettishly raised her tail in the air, so that the male *Capercaillies* could experience the whole meaning of its existence - namely the act of procreation.

Harald had almost cried when one of the hens had gotten wind of them and flew straight to the nearest male taking her out of her trance.

Soon after, the bird game play was over. Freddy had also come to his senses, and at Harald's talk the whole strange atmosphere disappeared - it was difficult for him to give any explanation as to why he did not want to shoot.

He said to Harald that it was a shame, that there were so few *Capercaillies* in Scotland and that the birds making the display were young birds, and that he had been waiting for an old one, one that would be OK to shoot. Harald accepted this, and Freddy helped him to shoot a huge one at a later display, and thus Harald was happy.

'Yes, you know', said Freddy. 'If they had a proper climate in Scotland, I don't think there is a nicer country. But since it's always raining, it will be tiring, at least when you're a sun worshipper like me.'

Knut had in the meantime opened the bottle of cognac and set about unwrapping the food, which turned out to be chicken. Knut didn't mention anything about what it had cost, and Freddy deliberately avoided getting into that subject. He was happy to give Knut the money that was left over.

He was completely convinced that Knut did not feel well financially these days and was always afraid that Knut would do something criminal. There had been a number of thefts and assaults since liberation, and every time Freddy read about such an assault where a mask and gun had been used, he thought of Knut and feared the worst.

CHAPTER 4

It was now late at night. The man who had met Freddy at the door had already gone home. He was one of the newer recruits in the Linge Company (The Linge Company was for a time among the most decorated military forces in The United Kingdom during World War II), and the three old veterans - as they felt - now got a really cosy sense of comradeship wash over them. It was as if everyone wanted to be nice to each other.

Knut had brought a whole loaf and butter and now set about cutting up the loaf and buttering it. The chickens were wrapped in some paper napkins.

It turned out to be five half chickens.

Knut regretted that he had not been able to get hold of more. He automatically assumed the role of host, set the table, extinguished the lights around the room, except at the particular table they were sitting at, and then he said, imitating the best English manner:

'Dinner is served'

Freddy and Harald sat down and then they toasted after Knut had welcomed them to the table.

All three threw themselves at the food. Harald, as if he had a fairly ordinary appetite; Knut seemed as if he was really starving, while Freddy thought to himself that maybe that was the case. Knut caught Freddy's eyes and suddenly said unmotivated:

'I have been begging for several days.'

'Cheers to Scotland!' said Harald. 'We were fools to complain when we were there.'

'Yes, we had no worries getting the daily bread', said Knut. Freddy took another piece of bread. After all, there were no more than five half-chickens, so he had to make do with one half, so there were two halves for the others. Knut needed it, while Harald could not understand why they could not divide equally or draw lots.

If Harald had really realised that Knut needed it, he would have been the first to give his share to Knut.

It's strange with men among themselves, but being able to go so far as to say that you are broke or begging is not easy. You don't want to arouse pity.

Since Knut himself had touched on those things, Freddy chose to get a little closer to his life and asked how it was going, if he had got a job? Knut sat with the chicken between both fists and with his elbows planted on the table as he gnawed on the meat. He put the chicken on the plate and took the glass with his greasy fingers.

'Toast!' he said. For some reason Freddy resented seeing the greasy fingers on the glass. The nails were long and with black, indelicate grooves, with the exception of the thumb and index finger where the nails were completely eaten away.

Knut took his toast very slowly, it looked like he was thinking about what he was going to say.

'You know, Freddy, it's not so easy for a guy like me. I never learned anything. I know you've had a varied life, but you've been out in the world. My childhood was always grey and sad, and due to poor financial conditions at home I had to start working for a general store as an errand boy before I finished school.'

'Yes, you know I've never had anything other than primary school. It was a bloody shitty job riding with goods until late at night. You can imagine for yourself that it wasn't always so fun to have to bring the goods into a house where perhaps the daughter in the house was a friend of yours from school, but she was in a position where the father could afford to let her continue her studies.'

'It wouldn't have been so dangerous if we had lived in an ordinary east-side quarter. But we lived a little outside the city in a so-called snob quarter, where people could be quite nasty to each other, and it is often said that similar children play best.'

'At least I always got that impression when I was a kid. I didn't belong among the other kids, in terms of clothes nor the environment, and I had to swallow a lot of shit.

My superior in the general store was basically quite decent, but when I later left him and started at another place which also included a room, things got harder. My predecessor had been a young boy who due to a lot of hard work and little and bad food, contracted tuberculosis. The food we got was the strangest food you could imagine.

Every time the general store received a lot of bananas, and they couldn't sell them all, the bananas became overripe and rotten, we could be sure that there would be banana soup for several days to come.

This was the case with most of the food we ate as it was the food that was leftover and unsaleable. The room where I stayed was a small room in a side building. In winter there was ice on the walls and the water in the jug to be used to wash myself would freeze when it was really cold.

But you know, shit, I got through it. But it's not so funny to admit that you have learned nothing but sabotaging and that all you know anything about is being an errand boy.

Harald now intervened in Knut's long speech:

'I think there is some nonsense with regard to being an errand boy. No one at school ever cares who you are - whether dad has money or not. And today, errand boys are actually in demand.'

Knut was starting to get a little drunk. He had made a voracious attack on the bottle as he had on the chicken.

'Oh shit!' he said, 'I could take a job as a helper again, but it's somehow a bit difficult to go back to such conditions after having tasted the finer world, as we did during the war.'

'Yes, you're absolutely right, think of me going to school again!'

Harald was not quite 20 years old when the war began, and had had to interrupt his studies. Throughout 1945 and 1946 he had only wandered and rattled, but his family had – even though his father was not wealthy – helped him to resume his studies.

'It is no fun having to live in a small room without a window and having to skip dinner for several days in a row. Every time I make a visit to the Club, I think of how I was a lieutenant back then and had a mistress in London, who had a car and nice things. I remember that I was actually a regular at one of the finest clubs in London, *The Four Hundred Club*. Admittedly, she was the one who had the money, but you know that when I came home from work I wasn't stingy either.'

'No, I keep repeating it to the point of boredom, what the hell were we complaining about when we were in England. We had it like the yolk in an egg. Just think of when we were in the English training camps and were woken up in the morning with tea by the bed brought by an over-polite slave of an attendant.'

'Your tea, Sir.'

'I felt like a King. On the whole, that life suited me perfectly. And a comparison to the English girls are not to be found on this earth.'

Knut began to sing in a slurred voice.

'When the girl is in bed then we are there', to the tune: *She'll be coming round the mountains.*

Both Knut and Freddy agreed. Harald continued the song by switching to the English lyrics:

'There'll be Hurricanes and Spitfires in the air'.

They sang the whole song and enjoyed themselves very much. They had become a little drunk - a little sad, and a little tired as they relived what once was, a very strange time; London in wartime.

They relived the atmosphere of many a night, with cute little English girls, plenty of money, nice people and good camaraderie. They could imagine Piccadilly with people singing and making love in the dark. Uniforms everywhere, and everyone who wore uniforms was the same. The English flight captain who was perhaps of noble descent, the Polish count, the Danish sailor and the Norwegian errand boy from the general store near Oslo.

Perhaps that night, while the air force fired the hardest at the German planes and the bombs rained down on London, they found each other and became like a big family despite the fact that they hardly understood each other. Perhaps the errand boy from Oslo found himself among twenty or thirty others at the home of a young lady, late at night, in a house that they had only read about in terms of wealth.

Was the errand boy perhaps bitter towards the rich in society? Did he find out here that in war, when it comes to be or not to be, it is the man that matters, and not what his father or family is?

Now they sat there singing and trying to live it all over again. But that time would never return. The friends they made during the war had slipped out of the picture, they didn't fit in peacetime, or maybe they themselves didn't fit them.

Their own very charming English had become bad English. When the smart uniform disappeared, the graduation suit appeared. It's even worse for the boys who got married, and who, in the belief that Norway would rise up only if the country became free, filled their English misses with stories that indicated that in Norway we were actually all landowners and wealthy.

It was not their fault that their imagination played tricks on them when they were constantly waiting to be killed, and it was not their fault that conditions became such after the war that to have been in England and fought for Norway had almost become a shame. At least that was the impression you got at the housing offices when it came to trying to get an apartment.

Freddy sat dozing and philosophising.

'Damn! now the bottle is empty', said Knut.

Well, then there was nothing to do but go home.

When they stood outside in the street they saw that the sky had cleared. As if on command all three began to relieve themselves while staring up at the stars. Nobody said anything. It was deathly quiet in the city. The sloshing from their streams sounded loudly in the night.

'Action Station!' Said Harald suddenly.

Freddy just stood there still thinking the same thing.

'Yes, isn't that strange', said Knut. 'Every time I look at the sky at night, I think of skydiving. I'm glad I don't have to do it again.'

We'll probably have to do it before too long, Harald thought suddenly.

'It's almost the same whatever the heck happens', Freddy replied, 'but I am glad that I'm not sitting in there', he said and pointed his head towards the gloomy outline of the huge prison.

'Yes, they will never get me in there again alive,' Knut said bitterly.

'But which way are you going? I'm going over to Torggaten - I have a girl I can sleep with tonight.'

As the others were going towards the west side, they parted:

'Thank you for a very lovely evening - so long.'

CHAPTER 5

Freddy wanted to be alone for a bit so he walked in a different direction than he originally planned. Harald shook his hand and thanked him by saying that he had not had such a good time for ages and that they must see each other more often. Freddy was happy when he saw Harald hurrying across the street, past the Justice Building towards Wergelandsveien.

Freddy strolled along towards Stortorget, he was tired. But all the same, he had become so restless that he knew it would be difficult to sleep.

On Stortorget, he went into a phone box. He put a coin in the phone, the dial tone came, but he thought again. He pressed the button and got the coin back.

It would be foolish to call her so late at night; he thought he should go home to his wife. He walked across the street, but then he quickly turned and went back to the phone box. He put the coin back in and waited for the dial tone and then dialled a number. He could hear the phone ringing and wondered what would happen next.

Suddenly a thought struck him:

- Imagine if she had a man with her!

He wanted to hang up, but then he heard her voice

on the other end of the line, a sleepy but clear voice saying:

'Hello?'

Freddy wanted to say something but it became just a mushy grunt. He cleared his throat and placed his hat next to the phone.

'Is that you Gerd?' he managed to say

'Yes!' answered the voice.

'It's Freddy.'

He heard the sleepiness disappear from the voice and it sounded agitated when she asked if something was wrong.

'No,' said Freddy, 'but I'm a bit out of balance and couldn't think of going home yet. Can you make me a cup of coffee?

'Come at once, I'll meet you at the gate. It's not worth waking up the whole house.'

'Where are you, by the way?'

Freddy said that he was at Stortorget, that there were no taxis at the stop and that he would probably take about fifteen minutes to walk up to where she lived in Parkveien.

'OK!' said the voice on the phone. 'I'm putting on the coffee now.'

Freddy hung up the phone, took his hat and stepped out of the phone box. A taxi stopped in the street, turned around and drove up to the taxi stop.

Freddy would rather walk and wandered out into the night. He looked at the clock; he wanted to be there in precisely fifteen minutes.

Thoughts began to swirl in his head about what could happen. He tried to force his thoughts into another direction. He thought of Gerd the way she was during the war, and what she had meant to him in his work.

He tried to imagine her as the good and fair companion who had shared good and bad with the boys. Little by little he noticed that the erotic wildness that had ignited in him at the thought of him going to her at this time of night began to subside and the feeling of comradeship took over.

A car suddenly slid silently up next to Freddy, and he jumped. His hand automatically went into his armpit to grip his gun.

Then he saw that it was a police patrol car. The car stopped and the two police officers sitting in front seat were staring at Freddy. The feeling of panic had completely seized him. He had a wild urge to run. He tried to reassure himself that there was no danger. This was August 1948, and the police officers were Norwegian – they weren't the Gestapo.

One of the policemen suddenly said:

'What the hell are you doing here in the middle of the night? Are you sabotaging?'

Then he laughed and said to the other policeman with a certain pride in his voice:

'This is Freddy, you've heard of him, right?'

The policeman held out a large fist and shook Freddy's hand. Freddy desperately tried to control the tremors in his mouth;

'Geez, how you scared me!'

The policeman had a good laugh.

'That was a good one, we managed to scare Freddy!'

'Oh, no, people like you don't have nerves at all, do they?'

'You can't have that can you?'

Freddy now remembered the policeman who had spoken to him. He had worked with him in the liberation days.

'I didn't recognise you right away,' Freddy said. 'How's it going?'

'Yes, you know I'm in the police. It's a bit of a pain, but it happens at night that we get to use some of what we learned from you. Besides, I'm sure it will probably break loose again soon.'

The other policeman laughed widely and said:

'Yes, you're probably the first to be picked up when they arrive, you have no chance at all.'

'No,' laughed Freddy, 'I guess I'll have to go underground again and start all over.'

'It's probably a question of whether you get a chance to get away. You have to count on them getting a false start, and they probably have their lists ready,' said the policeman whom Freddy knew.

'Which way are you going, by the way? You can jump in and we'll drive you.'

Freddy looked at the clock and thought of Gerd. Then he explained the way. The other policemen got out of the car and opened the back door.

'Jump in here!'

It gave Freddy a jolt when he realised that he had to enter the police car with the iron bars in front of the windows.

He hated the feeling of being locked up. It always reminded him of the time he had been kicked, half dead, into a police van by the Gestapo.

The big-fisted policeman snapped him out of his thoughts.

'How do you think it works in Berlin, Freddy? There will be a war. I don't see why they can't just start right away and be done with it. These hellish Russians want war no matter what the Allies are trying to do.'

'No, we should have continued directly towards

Moscow when they had taken Berlin. It's the same shit, communists and Nazis. Non of them are very wise. But I don't understand why the Americans can't drop nuclear bombs on Moscow and take down this Stalin?'

Freddy laughed a little.

'Yes, it's all a bit of a mess.'

'Yes, that's what I always say to Jensen.'

So his name is Jensen, Freddy thought.

'They should have sent over some fellows like you and the others. You would probably have cleaned up that Stalin and the whole mess.'

They arrived and Freddy thanked them for the drive. He looked at his watch, there were still three minutes left. The policemen looked like they wanted to continue talking, but Freddy waved so long, and took a few steps in the other direction. The car disappeared as Freddy turned and swung quickly across the street and headed towards an old four-story building. He saw that the door was slightly ajar, and then it opened.

It was Gerd.

'Morning,' she said. 'Be careful when walking in the hallway.'

Then they went up the stairs to the second floor. Here a door was open. Freddy noticed a business card that said Gerd Dyrup.

Call three times, was typed under the name. Above the business card was a very ostentatious brass sign, where under the name was written *Office Manager*. Freddy sneaked in, and Gerd carefully closed the door.

There was a strange musty smell in the hall, a mixture of old furniture and apples. There was a very large mirror in the hall and Freddy could now see himself in the dim light from a room where the door was open and where there was a dim light. Gerd put a finger to her mouth and pulled him after her across the hall towards the open door. Freddy walked in.

Gerd closed the door and breathed a sigh of relief.

'Now we are saved, for this time,' she added out of old habit. 'Here we can talk. The others sleep on the other side of the hall. By the way, they are so good, I had something to do with them during the war. He was one of our secret 'mailboxes' or places where we could leave our messages, while someone else could pick them up without anyone knowing, or connect us.'

'We had to send him to Sweden at the end of the war. His wife ended up at Grini Prison, but thank God, it saved their lives. Their apartment was burgled, we managed to recover most of the stolen goods afterwards, but you know they lost a lot. And you yourself know what compensation they receive from the state. It's sickening to see him walking around in a suit that you can see right through. Always freshly pressed and cared for. The shirts are always clean and I know it's just a matter of time before the shirts don't reach below the trouser belt due to her constantly having to cut pieces off the shirt to make shirt collars.'

'But that wasn't what we were supposed to talk about. The coffee isn't finished yet. The damn plate takes so long to heat up. If you fancy a smoke, I have some American here that I got hold of. It's your special brand *Lucky Strike*. Was it not *lucky pacifiers,* or something like that you usually called them, to speak slang?'

Freddy took a cigarette and looked around while Gerd took out a couple of glasses and a bottle of white Curacao.

'I got this from an uncle the day before yesterday, who thought I deserved it when I had saved the family's honour. He is such a cuddly old darling who likes to talk about the resistance 24 hours a day if he gets the chance. Every time there is an informant who gets away with a prison sentence, he comes up to me. He then likes to have a small sip from the bottle. I then make coffee while he babbles about how awful it is that they can't all be shot.'

'His standing argument is that they, the informants, were sentenced to death during the war and were listed by the Royal Norwegian Government in London, while the high lords in London let our handsome boys become assassins.'

Gerd strikingly imitated an old man's voice:

'It was like saying that when it was militarily important, you are not allowed to let such pigs live, just because the Norwegian people have been fed with a loud of lies and don't understand that we may have to go through it all again.'

Freddy laughed.

'I know the type, Gerd - more blood for the money. Now the coffee is boiled.'

The room felt cosy, which was a combined kitchen and bedroom. He saw that Gerd had put a blanket over the large sofa bed.

It was as if Gerd read his thoughts.

She said:

'You must excuse me, but I actually didn't bother to dress properly.'

Freddy looked at Gerd. She had thrown on a tight-fitting dressing gown with a belt around her waist. He let his gaze slide down her figure with relish. How beautifully she was made. She seemed so small and feminine as she shuffled around in morning slippers and tended to the coffee and found some cakes in a box in the cupboard.

Poor little one, it probably wasn't easy to be her either.

'Is it going well at work, Gerd?'

'Yes, you know it's hard, but I guess I'll have to hold

out for a while longer.'

Gerd was employed at Victoria Terrasse after he war. (Victoria Terrasse was the Gestapo's headquarters in Oslo during the Second World War. The place had an interrogation room and was used, among other things, for interrogation and torture of Norwegians who were imprisoned by the German occupying power.)

It was as if she didn't want to lose touch with what once was. But by all accounts she had tired of the whole court settlement a long time ago.

It was as if Gerd sensed his thoughts.

She poured the coffee and said:

'You know it was interesting at the beginning, we were all enthusiastic and saw it as a task to get this settlement done as quickly as possible and as fairly as possible.'

'I think it was a colossal mistake that we tried to punish everyone. We should have concentrated on those who were really guilty. All the dangerous whistle-blowers, all the big ones who had really failed, all those who had had the intelligence to understand that what they were doing was wrong. I can't help the fact that I often think it is unfair to judge a person as a traitor to the country, who for idealistic reasons has been a member of the *NS (Nasjonal Samling - The Nazi Political Party in Norway during its occupation)*. Now don't misunderstand me, it is clear that members of the *NS* are criminally liable. But let's be honest, it was difficult in 1940 and later they were frozen out by the rest of us. I think we made a big mistake by not trying to convert them during the war. But you know that a Nazi during the war never got a chance to be a honourable man. He could leave the party as much as he wanted. He was branded and his children had to go through all sorts of problems at school. He was frozen out everywhere. His whole family, including the young children, had to suffer because their father had been a Nazi. The rest of us could buy on the black market. We could make arrangements with the merchant if there was a possibility. But the little insignificant *NS* man, he and his whole family had to get by on their rations. There were rarely any relatives in the country who sent them any food, except in those cases where there was a farmer in the family who was also *NS*.

'No, I always regret that we didn't give more of them a chance to work for us.'

Freddy poured some Curacao into the glasses.

'You're a bit wrong there, Gerd. You mustn't forget everything we had to deal with from those people, and how the hell did you want us to be able to trust them - usually they where untrustworthy and unsympathetic?'

'Today we talk about the front fighters as if they were martyrs. Have you forgotten the scum-bag 'Norwegian SS' (Norwegian defectors that had joined the German SS within Norway) who checked you on the street the same day Erik was shot? I see you're blushing just at the thought.

What would you say if one of them stood in your office one day and rattled off the usual lesson that he thought Norway's salvation was through the *NS,* and that it was against the communists that he had fought?'

'Have you forgotten the *Shepard boys*' (hirdguttenes) mob behaviour? Have you forgotten the *Corporate Security Defence* who walked around Oslo's streets with their finger on the trigger, wanting to shoot - just to become like proper soldiers? You've probably forgotten - and maybe that's the right thing - but it's not always that easy.'

Gerd had become eager. He recognised her wartime eagerness.

'Oh, Freddy, I know you're right. You mustn't think that I am not committed. - but sometimes I actually don't know what to believe. It's all so unfair. I have seen how small *NS* members, after serving their sentence, have desperately tried to get a job. And when they have finally managed to trick their way into a workplace, the workers have threatened to strike and forced them out again as soon as it was discovered that they had been in the *NS.*

'And the worst screamers have often been those who worked for the Germans during the war. I have never been able to understand why the German workers should not be punished. Think of the many thousands of workers who went from their good jobs to the Germans because it was better paid. Were they not guilty of punishment? Wasn't that helping the enemy? And they go completely free, and

53

not only that, but they should be able to judge these little miserable individuals, whose great crime has been that they belonged to the National Assembly and did not understand enough to get out of it all.'

'Don't you think it is terrible that we have not yet heard of anyone who has been punished because they worked at German facilities. Do you remember the workers who helped the Germans load bombs into the planes at Værnes Airport near Trondheim in 1940, when the Germans bombarded our own forces in the north? Have you ever heard of them being punished?'

'Toast!' said Freddy. 'Let's talk about something else. It's no use discussing those things, it's complete bullshit! I had thought that there would be a court-martial and that several officers who failed would lose their heads.'

'But now I don't understand anything. I basically also agree with you regarding the small *NS* members. It seems that they and only they will pay the debt.'

'But it's hopeless now, the whole thing. I have given up thinking about what treason entails. It seems to me that if you can say: "I didn't know that", or "I didn't understand that", then you could actually allow yourself to do anything, both to give orders not to fight and to directly help the Germans.'

'But for God's sake let's talk about something else. How are things going with the three young terrorists you got hold of?'

Gerd took a sip from her glass.

'I don't know if you know anything more about the case, Freddy, but I can tell you that it's no joke. You know I have nothing to do with that matter, but I have now had a bit of a sniff. It is not for nothing that I work at Victoria Terrasse.'

'The three young boys had sworn to avenge the father of one of the boys, who is therefore the main man. He is the son of the terrible informer whom you remember was executed in his own garden in 1944 near…. Yes, what was it called?'

Freddy recalled the name.

'Right,' said Gerd. 'As far as I understand, the three boys also have a clue as to who the Rat Catcher was.'

Freddy drained his glass and poured himself another. He then lit a cigarette, took a deep drag and as he followed the smoke with his eyes he said:

'I am sometimes surprised by how much you know, and I am convinced that you learned most of it after the war. There are many indications that there is a leak somewhere.'

'And when you're so rude that you only help yourself, I guess I'll have to pour myself some,' said Gerd.

Freddy apologised smilingly and poured for her. He slowly felt that he was getting pleasantly drunk.

'Basically I'm a fool,' he suddenly said to Gerd. 'Here I sit alone with the world's cutest girl, it's late in the morning and I'm just sitting here talking coldly.'

He thought that Gerd blushed a little, but she quickly answered with jargon:

'Yes, adorable, absolutely delicious, isn't it?'

And in the same breath:

'Don't start such nonsense Freddy. Our friendship is far too precious to be ruined by something like this that you just say because you've been drinking.'

'You're right Gerd, forget it! But I guess I have to make it home. You also have to go to work tomorrow.'

'You are welcome to stay here until tomorrow morning if you want. There are only a couple of hours left, but it's quite uncomfortable here.'

'I think it's best that I go anyway,' said Freddy.

He got up, took his hat and coat.

'Maybe I am, after all, a fool?'

Gerd looked at him a little strangely, then she carefully opened the door and sneaked across the hall to the entrance door, which she carefully opened.

Freddy followed her to the front door. Gerd opened it:

'Yes, good night Freddy, and remember that you can

always call me at any time of the night, and even if I don't always have a kind uncle giving me a bottle, I can always offer you coffee. And if you feel that you need some disconnection - just come up.'

'Oh Freddy, please, be careful. You have to reckon that there are some vengeful souls out there that it might click for one day, and they are stronger and more organised than you think.'

Freddy looked down at her. He felt a wild desire to take her in her arms, caress her little face, carry her in his arms over to the covered sofa and fall to rest, close to her.

With a jerk he tore himself free.

'Thanks for the tip Gerd, but I'm not convinced. It was nice of you to see me tonight. I'll see you another day.'

And then he quickly went out into the street, without looking back.

He now felt that it was all perfect.

He was the world's loneliest person. Even she had not understood him. But did he really understand himself? Wasn't he just an incorrigible daydreamer—and didn't he love to go around feeling sorry for himself? Did other people do the same? Did they also go around playing big melodramas for themselves. Couldn't he just concentrate on what was going on in his country?

Why did it bother him that many of the people he met in the restaurants in the evening were war profiteers?

Why did it bother him that so many people had grown up during the war sat at home on their bums and took advantage of the opportunities that had been created by a lot of young, brave people that gave their everything for Norway, including their education, their nervous system and their lives?

After all, he couldn't expect people to go around feeling sorry for him because he, with his vivid imagination, imagined that one day he would be the victim of an assassination by a vengeful soul. After all, he felt that Gerd was right in what she said about the three young boys who had been arrested after they had carried out a foolish bombing attack on a well-known person, which had only resulted in insignificant, material damage.

But Freddy had got the big shake when he had actually been shot at a few months after liberation. What lay behind it, he did not know. No one knew, except the two fellows who carried it out, and they had gotten away. But the memory of it and the certainty that it could happen again at any time, no matter what time of day or night, had probably contributed to his often dark outlook on life. He thought it unfair that the airmen and the soldiers were done with the war and its anxiety, while he had to toil on with his sweaty fingers on the pistol grip, always on guard, always prepared to be fired upon. And he felt how unfair it was that no one had wanted to take responsibility for the rat catching after the war. Those who had given the orders had probably never thought of how complicated it could become after the war.

Freddy had never thought about what it would mean to carry out an order to really delete a name on the list, and then discover that behind that name on a piece of paper was hiding a fanatical but confused Nazi.

Now there was only an old, more or less harmless fellow, whose only armament consisted of an umbrella, and who stood there fumbling as he muttered: 'What is this all about?' and then only fell on the third or fourth shot.

That memory would never go away. It would surely follow him for the rest of his life, reminding him of the fellow who had told him once, when he was on holiday in Stockholm, that he wouldn't shake his hand, because, as he said, he wouldn't shake a murderer's hand.

After all, this episode wasn't the worst Freddy had experienced. He had been horrified that the fellow knew about his work, and he had been wounded to the core by suddenly discovering that someone could see it that way.

At that time he had driven up to *Auntie,* (The nickname of Ida Bernardes, Max's future wife), who was the link between the English and the Norwegians in the British Legation). Here he had said that he was going home immediately. He had not answered the question about the reason for the hasty departure. He had just arrived broken down in Stockholm after a job which had been very nerve-racking and which had cost many Norwegian lives in reprisals. In the end he had given in to *Auntie's* pressure and told the story of the handshake. He was completely broken. *Auntie* had, however, got him on the right track again. She had said he had the cleanest hands and had kissed both of his hands.

Once, after such a meeting, he had gone straight out into the street, had driven up to the English embassy and asked to be sent back home to Norway immediately.

The English had tried to find out the reason, but Freddy had kept tight-lipped and just said he wanted to go back home.

The man he had spoken to had understood that something was wrong, because Freddy had just come over to Sweden to get a hard-earned rest and holiday. The last job he in Norway had cost many Norwegian lives in reprisals, and the Englishman had understood that there was something weighing on Freddy. He had made Freddy come home with him, and here he had poured as much liquor into Freddy as he could swallow.

He drunk himself completely unconscious, for three days he just lay there drinking. He had barely managed to crawl out of bed and into the toilet.

He later understood that they had let him drink himself out of his sanity and concentration - because they actually believed that he was ripe for a nervous breakdown, and that it might be better if he knocked himself out with drink.

A nervous breakdown had not come and Freddy had slowly returned to earth again, but after that he constantly feared having a breakdown. Now he was in a sad period of his life, but still had to try and free himself from his tragic situation.

CHAPTER 6

Freddy discovered that the trams had started to run, and he jumped on one that was going to Majorstuen. Workers who had been on night shifts were now on their way home, and other early pedestrians had begun to appear in the streets.

At *Vibesgate*, Freddy jumped off the tram, at the gate he found the key and let himself into an old tenement. He went up the dreary stairs, all the way to the fourth floor. There was a sign that read: *Hans Olsen, Tram Conductor.*

It was only this sign, as Freddy himself did not have one. Those who came to him rang three times and the postman recognised him.

There was a bad smell in the hall, much like a bad smell of fish. Freddy sighed, unlocked the door and entered the apartment. The bad smell from the hallway followed him, it was now mixed with a penetrating smell of paint.

Freddy remembered that Olsen had been talking for a long time about painting the kitchen, which was absolutely terrifying. He heard someone turn over in bed in the room directly off the entrance hall.

Then he heard a voice calling faintly:

'Freddy, is that you?'

Freddy didn't bother to answer. He closed the door

behind him and opened the door into the room where the voice came from.

The room was dimly lit from the bedside lamp. A large double bed took up almost the entire room, and the first impression was that the rest of the space in the room was occupied by mirrors and toilet articles. Next to the bed was a huge radio. On the wall above the bed hung a machine gun and a dagger, such as the commandos used. There was also a German officer's dagger hanging on the wall. Below these weapons hung several diplomas, which on closer inspection turned out to be military awards, and to which the medals were attached. There were two of the highest Norwegian war decorations you could get, as well as two English ones which were actually a rare treat to get from such a country.

As these accolades caught his eye Freddy repeated to himself his old promise:

'Tomorrow I will take them down.'

Because this is what he had said to himself almost every single night lately when he got home.

But they were still there.

He could well remember the day he came home and discovered that Miriam had hung them on the wall. Actually, at first he had become embarrassed, but when he saw her joy having made the room as cosy as she said, he had not been able to bear to hurt her.

Now Miriam sat in bed and looked at him without saying a word. Freddy, even in this moment where he deeply hated the thought of her, had to admit that she looked good.

Miriam was blonde, but to become even blonder she had bleached her hair, and the result was extreme. However, in the broad daylight when they were out together meeting acquaintances, it wasn't so bad. But perhaps not everyone thought like him.

And not so long ago he himself had been completely blind to everything when it came to Miriam. And, he had to admit, that here at home right now, in the more intimate evening light, she was wonderful to look at. Her angry-like temperament made her eyes sparkle and glow. Her big hair stood like a golden cloud around her head.

She had a fiery red, beautifully shaped, perhaps a little too big mouth, Freddy had to smile when he realised that she had obviously put her lipstick on when she heard the door slam.

But now Miriam was furious. Her eyes were wide. She was wearing a very low-cut nightgown, and one of her breasts had slipped out of the dress. It suddenly struck Freddy and he took pity on Miriam, but at least it was possible to buy bras that gave a great bust out of nothing. And think what hair she would have had if women had not been able to dye and curl their hair.

Miriam was what many would call beautiful. But

there was something unspeakably cheap about her. Her naturally beautiful bust was marred by the fact that she lifted her breasts up with a smart American brassiere. Her dresses were always too challenging, but she was also the type a soldier dreams of when he has lived an abnormal life for a long time. Everything about her was lush and inviting.

But as perfect as her body was, she didn't have much to show in her head.

Freddy had met her during a period when he himself was far from normal. And the complete, maddening, erotic dependence on her that he had fallen into had resulted in them now being married.

But as everyday life had sunk in, the more he knew it couldn't work.

Deep down, he had actually known that, from the beginning. In any case from the moment they had stood there and promised each other to be faithful in good times and bad, the whole madness was only based on erotica and they really had nothing to say to each other. They lived on separate globes and in separate air bubbles. Sex and eroticism are only nourished if other common values are also allowed to develop. Mind and soul must also be fed.

Therefore, this marriage had no basis. But now they were married, and her erotic wildness helped him through many a terrible moment when his melancholy and depression were breaking him.

The worst part was that in reality he had started to use her in the same way as one uses artificial means - as if she were a sleeping pill. Strangely enough, he was never disgusted by her at night, but much more so in the morning and during the day. She was undeniably the type who belonged to the night. She loved to lie about all day and then become alive during the evening and night.

Freddy cleared his throat slightly, then said:

'Can I open the window a little? You know I don't sleep well if I don't get fresh air?'

Of course he got no answer.

When he got to the window, there was a deep plate there with something in it that turned out to be meatballs. Now, with the light on, and the congealed fat with the onion on top, it looked completely unappetising.

He moved the meatballs even though he didn't immediately know where to put them. He placed them on the low dressing table. Even there, he first had to move some pots of creams, most of which were without lids.

Suddenly Miriam began to speak. Crackling, stormy, like from a machine gun. From where he stood, full of guilty conscience, he had to admit that she had, in one way, become even more beautiful.

But he couldn't say that.

'Aren't you ashamed?' she continued furiously. But at the same time she looked terribly sad. The tears, mixed with dark mascara, began to run like sharp furrows down her face. It looked almost grotesque.

Freddy sighed to himself. For now he suddenly felt that everything was more hopeless than ever.

She continued:

'Here I have sat and waited for you for hour after hour, and I had…' Her voice broke and the crying became even more violent. She tried to control herself. But now everything had gotten so far that it was simply hopeless:

'And I who had prepared such a cosy evening for us! I had got hold of meat, I decorated, and managed to get some homemade cosy candles.'

As he had feared, she exploded in a rage that made him even more miserable:

'Do you believe it's funny to almost have to sleep with the butcher to get meat? And not to mention the struggle to cook - I've been sitting here like an idiot whilst you've been out and about with other girls!'

'But now you can swear it will end! I also know where to go if I feel like having fun!' Her voice had now become screechy and shrill and Freddy began to think about the man they rented the flat from. At the same time he knew that Miriam was now working herself up to full hysteria.

He went over to her, took her by the wrist and squeezed:

'Shut up,' he said brutally. 'Are you planning to wake up the whole building?'

Miriam tried to bite his hand. Freddy calmly took her hair with his other hand.

'Calm down Miriam - let me explain. I have been very busy and I've earned a lot of money.'

He saw that, that worked. When she started to calm down, he let her go and sat down next to her on the bed. Freddy stroked her hair as Miriam laid down sobbing, burying her head in the pillow.

'So, my little treasure, I'm sorry, but I just couldn't let you know.'

Miriam spoke into the quilt:

'Oh Freddy, you are so cruel to me! I'm not used to this, and I was really looking forward to tonight. I had a lot of red wine and even got hold of a bottle of champagne for us to enjoy.' She sobbed again, 'you didn't come!'

'Yes, but now I have arrived,' said Freddy, 'and I am very hungry. Let's party now!'

Miriam got up in bed:

'Is it true that you have don business and that you have not been unfaithful?'

'I swear,' said Freddy.

Then he kissed her on the cheek.

'Do you think I have such a tremendous capacity?' he added jokingly.

'Where's the champagne?'

He spotted it in the corner by the radio. He took two beer glasses out of the cupboard, but then Miriam jumped out of bed and gleefully retrieved two champagne glasses which she teasingly held up in the air:

'Look what I managed to get for our house!'

Freddy pulled her close to him. She slid passionately up to him and kissed him, holding the glasses far from her with one hand.

Freddy – still kissing her – let himself fall onto the bed.

Miriam broke free:

'Watch the glasses, you fool!'

Freddy grabbed her again.

'No, wait Freddy, you know that you'll just fall asleep and I won't be able to wake you up again.'

'We're going to enjoy ourselves properly.'

Freddy opened the bottle with a bang

'Now the landlord probably thinks I shot you,' he laughed.

He felt himself getting into a relaxed mood and toasted Miriam. He suddenly felt hungry and now the thought of the meatballs were delicious. He gorged them with the fat and onions and boasted greatly of them and of her. He toasted her cooking skills and made a silly little speech for the big day.

The champagne bottle was soon empty and Miriam found a bottle of brandy from which she supplied herself richly.

Freddy also took his share, and felt that now he was really starting to get drunk and tired. He took off his jacket, tore off the shoulder holster with the gun, hung the holster up next to the bed and laid the gun on the table. He undid his belt and let his trousers slide to the floor. He kicked off his shoes and left everything where it was. He threw his shirt on the chest of drawers, then he let his underpants slide down, kicking them off with his feet as he tore off his vest. He used his hands to remove his socks.

He was now completely naked. He took off his wristwatch and automatically wound it up and placed it next to the gun on the bedside table.

Miriam had jumped back into bed and had put the glass next to her on the bedside table.

'I'll use the pot,' said Freddy. 'I don't want to go all the way down the hall.'

After using the pot, he got back into bed and reached for the glass he had placed next to him on the bedside table.

'Cheers, Miriam! At least we get on well with each

other now and then. At least now,' he said and kissed her.

The kiss stirred him up, he put the glass down and got close to her. She reached out and turned off the light on her bedside lamp. He did the same to his as he heard her take off her nightgown. He lay down close to her warm body and caressed her, forgetting all her faults. He forgot that basically he had never felt anything but erotic fascination for her. He actually forgot that it was her, and suddenly it was as if it was Gerd he was caressing! That was how strong his imagination was.

Afterwards he only felt the wonderful feeling that he was now able to sleep; sleep away all the difficulties and evil, sleep away the grey everyday life, sleep with peace of mind; and forget - forget everything.

CHAPTER 7

Freddy opened his eyes and was suddenly wide awake. He heard a door being opened, and a voice - which he understood to be Mrs Olsen's. She spoke to someone at the door. The door was closed with a bang, and the steps continued up to the next floor and he then heard a doorbell ring.

So it had been someone door selling. Freddy was dozing and almost falling asleep again. Half asleep, his thoughts went back to when he was a young boy selling flowers at the door, in that terrible time when it was impossible for a young boy without acquaintances to get work. It was impossible to get into an apprenticeship.

Young people struggled in the workplaces. Even those with a good education had long days with so-called starter salaries of NOK 50-60 (4/5 pounds sterling) a month.

Freddy had made a good profit from his door to door selling. But he had had to swallow his pride when he met schoolmates, who, because of better-off parents, were able to continue their education or could have an office position at the ridiculous salary of NOK 50-60 a month because they lived at home for free and could use this salary as pocket money.

However, that time had not lasted that long. Freddy

had got a job on the sea as a greaser, and had later risen a little in the ranks.

He had tried all aspects of sea life, both in the engine room and on deck.

He had also been a beggar in Buenos Aires. He had worked in the jungles of Central America. He had experienced a great adventure and fallen madly in love with the wife of the chief of police in one of the large labour camps, where the mines were located - where copper is extracted in Chilé.

Freddy had been very young. Everything was exciting and fine - until the husband of his beloved was suddenly stood at the bedroom door. Freddy had literally jumped out of the window, and to this day he didn't understand how he had managed to take his trousers with him. He had heard gunfire crack behind him, and the bullets had blown up yellow dust in the road where he ran for his life.

Freddy understood that he had misunderstood the situation a little. He was in a country where it is not only natural, but that a man with a little pride certainly had to be unfaithful; it was men's prerogative. But it was unforgivable that a married woman was unfaithful.

Now, Freddy had quickly gotten over the loss of the hot-blooded police chief's wife. It was much worse that he had to run away from everything he owned in the world, except for the shirt and the trousers that had been saved at the last minute.

Freddy was young, his life was ahead of him, he had no idea what war was; the sun was shining; fruit cost nothing - and after all he had come into this life without shoes.

The years passed. Freddy did well. He learned to use his hands. He took jobs that paid well, jobs that others didn't want. Deep in Columbia's jungle or high up in the mountains. In gold mines, where the only access was by plane. He saved up quite considerable sums in US dollars, and learned good habits when he was in civilised areas.

Then he made, what he often said to himself was the biggest mistake of his life: he travelled back to Norway.

He quickly had enough of Norway, but before he could get out again, the war came.

He was ashamed of being a Norwegian in the April of 1940. He walked around and slept until he saw the men in Oslo on the panic day, when everyone lost their minds. Then he travelled up one of the valleys to try to get together with some men who wanted to fight.

He had been among the more fortunate who did not have to go and be ashamed for the rest of his life. He came into battle. Since then he had automatically entered into resistance work and been treated badly by the Germans when it was his turn to be arrested.

In captivity he had an opportunity to escape and did not give a damn about the call that no one should escape so as not to harm the others.

He had ended up in England and joined the SOE (Special Operation Executive) where he received hard training and learned everything about sabotage and liquidation. He had enjoyed life and later had enjoyed the thrill of sabotage. He had also discovered that he was, after all, more fond of his country than most others.

He had regained faith in the Norwegian people through the unprecedented unity during the war years. Despite his changing life - or perhaps precisely because of it - he had never learned a proper subject. Now he was married he had to get up and go to a job.

Freddy looked at his wristwatch that was lying on the table - half past twelve.

'Damn!' he said. He looked at Miriam as she lay sleeping. She lay half naked, the covers had slipped off her. The wart on her breast was like an evil eye staring at him.

He felt a sudden disgust for her.

He stood up. He looked at the mess. His clothes were in a pile on the floor, the rest of the meatballs made him feel sick. He got dressed, put his gun in the holster, enabled the safety catch and made his way to the door. He stopped, went back and got his toothbrush.

He breathed in the fresh air as he stood on the street. He headed towards Majorstuen and into a barber's shop. He had to wait a while, the barber gave him the day's paper.

There it was written with huge headlines that the

Russians had closed the American consulates in Russia and their own in America. President Truman had now withdrawn the Russian envoy's credentials. Another headline reported that the four-power meeting in Moscow had broken down. Further down it said that the American spokesman had stated that the Americans feared the worst but hoped for the best, and that all hope was not lost yet.

Freddy lit a cigarette.

The barber said to him:

'Yes, now hell must break loose?'

Freddy took a long drag before answering:

'God knows what they will do in Berlin in a month's time, when they can no longer maintain the flight connection.'

The man whom the barber was attending intervened in the conversation by saying:

'Yes, it will probably be the same thing again. No, you should get away. I spent three years in Germany, and that will be enough for the rest of my life. I have little desire for Siberia.'

The barber stopped shaving, struck out his hand and said:

'I spent eight months in *Grini Prison*. It wasn't as bad as in Germany, but I'm saying the same thing. I have little desire for Siberia. What the hell do we do?'

'No, if I could get to America, I'd leave tomorrow.'

'I hope to leave in six weeks, then I will have my visa and say goodbye to Norway,' said the man sitting in the chair.

'Yes, there are some lucky ones,' said the barber resignedly.

'Here it will probably just be toil and pay taxes. When you have finally paid the tax, the Russians will come - then you will end up in Siberia! If it hadn't been so expensive, I would have closed the shop and gone home and got drunk when I saw the headlines in the paper today. And meanwhile the bourgeois and labour press quarrel and prepare for elections. I would like to see them choose when the Russians have occupied our country. No, we should have had a man like *Churchill* here. He would have tidied up the whole thing. It would be great to have him as the Minister of Defence.'

'He has met him,' said the barber suddenly, pointing at Freddy and addressed the man in the chair:

'This gentleman is one of the saboteurs who was at the castle and got to greet *Churchill*,' he said explanatory.

The man looked into the mirror and waved his hand:

'You did well. I was so damn unlucky. I never got anything done. I was caught for some nonsense and ended up in Germany. Tell me, what was *Churchill* like?'

'He was a very nice fellow, said Freddy. Just like you

see him in the movies.'

To himself he thought:

Who can tell what *Churchill* was really like? He was so larger than life. He, who through five long years was more than God had ever been to Freddy. He had tears in his eyes just thinking about the great man, the one who, when it mattered, when it really mattered, had saved the world.

Freddy had not been able to understand that it was true that he would experience the happiness of breathing the same air as *Churchill*. He understood afterwards that it was King Haakon who had wanted some of the leading saboteurs to greet *Churchill*.

It had been without comparison the greatest moment of his life when he got to shake *Churchill's* hand. He thought he felt that the great statesman perceived that these fellows gathered around him, in spite of all the disappointments and weariness they had experienced after liberation, were willing to fight again if he or the king went ahead and called for battle again. He could have told the man in the chair that he had gone out afterwards and kissed his hand where *Churchill's* hand had touched him, but you don't say that.

Freddy did not push it into anything more in his description than that *Churchill* was a very nice fellow.

The man in the chair was done and Freddy sat down. As he went Freddy wished him good luck in America. After he was shaved he walked over to a taxi and gave an address. A while later, the taxi stopped in a street not far from *Akerselven*.

Freddy paid and walked across the street. He unbuttoned his jacket so he could quickly get to his gun, and entered a gate. A sign stated that there was a car body shop in the yard. Freddy walked in. There were three guys working there.

'Morning,' said Freddy. 'Is this where the action takes place?'

A big strong guy came towards Freddy. He dried his hands with a rag. He seemed to be in bad spirit:

'Freddy, it's some damn shit working with such bad materials which we use. You know that the primer that we smear on these cars is worth nothing, and the varnish we spray on is going to fall off in a short time. It's pure fraud.'

Freddy took a match he had lying loose in his pocket, put it in his mouth and began to chew on it. He spat out a stub and said, pushing his hat to the back of his neck:

'Come with me to the office Anders.'

The paint shop was a large garage that had been fitted out as a workshop. There was only room for three cars inside at the same time, so they always had cars parked in the courtyard. The office consisted of a small cubicle lined with veneer sheets. The room was furnished with two chairs and a desk, as well as a small safe. There was a half-full and an empty milk bottle on the desk. On the wall hung two pictures, one of the king and one of *Churchill*.

'Sit down,' Freddy said to Anders. 'Have a cigarette.'

Anders took a cigarette. Freddy lit it up and took one for himself.

'Let's face the truth,' he continued. 'All the work done by garages is only first class when it comes to the bills. You know that today it actually costs around NOK 1400 to have an ordinary American 85-horsepower engine drilled and overhauled. Painting an ordinary 5-seater comes at around a thousand. If the car is to have new seat covers inside, it will cost another thousand - and then the work is of poor quality.'

'It's difficult to blame the workshops. After all, the large workshops mainly deal with apprentices. The skilled repairmen start workshops for themselves in the countryside and elsewhere. Such small workshops also try to get hold of car wrecks that they can fix, and then they repaint them in small specialist workshops like ours before they go on the black market. It's all well and good if there weren't such phenomenal prices for the cars, but you yourself know what is paid, and we are – whether we like it or not – a part of the whole thing. Even if we try to do proper work, it is impossible to get good materials, so we have to take what we get and make the best of it. The only consolation I can give you is that we do the job better than most.'

Anders moved his heavy body a little. The chair

creaked.

'It's clear that it's non of my business Freddy, but I think it is sad to do a bad job, and it does not pay off in the long term.'

Freddy was annoyed.

'What the hell do you want me to do Anders? It is not me who imports varnish and primer. Besides, it's a question of whether there are any decent things left in this damned world at all. Look at this crap desktop here. I bought it from Erling for, I think it was over NOK 400. Double what I could ever in my wildest dreams imagine it was worth.'

Anders looked at the desk. It was a fairly ordinary small desk in light oak veneer with three drawers on each side, and a central drawer. Freddy had to get up and actually walk out of the little cubicle every time he wanted to open them, because they were so idiotically placed and were in the way of the person who was going to use the table. It was an ordinary idiotic desk of the kind that was manufactured everywhere, and had looked the same for the last hundred years.

'I'm so pissed off with this crap table,' Freddy continued.

'The drawers always stick. They can scarcely be moved. Soon I'll be planing them off every other day.'

'Look at this,' he said and pulled out one of the

drawers. 'It has now become so weak and ugly from all the planing. I was so pissed off last time that I planed off way too much, just to know that at least I could get them in and out, instead of pushing and shoving.'

'But enough about that and more about something else. I just want you to understand that creating first class work is like hitting the wall. Making anything will soon be impossible. You know that Erling runs this factory that made this desk. He works together with Willy and Egil, and you won't believe what they say about the pace of work and the quality of the work, Erling and Egil have had to forbid Willy from showing up at the factory anymore. You know he has such a bloody temper, and when he came down to the factory one day and found that three of the guys were drunk and two had gone home in the middle of working hours, then you know he blew up. The result was one hell of a ballad. The three fellows had told Willy to go to hell, and not to interfere in their affairs, otherwise he could do the job himself. There were plenty of jobs to get! Willy may not always be a quick thinker, but he strikes all the more quickly. You remember that night in Durban?'

Anders grinned. But here the situation had become the same. Egil had come driving into the courtyard some time after the noise started. His description was that it looked awful out there. As he said – German-workers were plastered all over the walls. And in the middle of it all, Willy sat on the back of a huge guy and twisted his foot around until he lay snotty and had to say according to Willy's dictation: 'I'm a damned German-worker, and I'm going to learn to shut up.'

Anders laughed. He had been with Willy in a unit of the Norwegian Navy, which had been stationed in *Durban* in South Africa. They had been doing mine-sweeping, and he himself was no small boy and had vivid memories of the last fight in which he had been in because of Willy.

It had cost him a new false tooth.

'He probably got into a lot of trouble afterwards, I can imagine?'

'I don't know,' said Freddy, 'but I assume so. In any case, he must stay away from the factory. It doesn't matter what type of worker they get in there. As Soon as Willy discovers that they have been drinking during working hours or not kept the tempo, he accuses them of being German-workers, after that the trouble starts.'

'Nowadays, he is passing the time on breaking the legs of half the Home Guard. You know he has become an instructor in jiu-jitsu for the Home Guard?'

'I'm also in the Home Guard,' said Anders, 'but it is in a different area.'

The phone rang. Freddy picked it up, looked at his wristwatch and said:

'OK, so we say three o'clock on *Telle?*'

'It was Erling,' said Freddy. 'I meet him at *Telle* at

three o'clock. I wonder if he got us some barracks?'

'Geez, you can be sure that Erling will sort it out, if he can earn something from it. He's always keen on money.'

'Yes,' said Freddy, 'he is very smart, and he knows everyone. But I think I'll sneak away and have a sauna bath, last night became very heavy.'

He took his hat:

'Don't think about it any more with regard to the priming. You see Anders, there is nothing better to get hold of.'

Anders shrugged his heavy shoulders:

'No, you know, I give a damn! It's just that it's more fun to work when you have good things to do it with. But forget it! Say hello to Erling.'

Freddy walked out, but then suddenly turned around:

'Anders, can I borrow the car this afternoon?'

'Just take it,' Anders said. 'It's in the parking lot - here's the key.'

Freddy grabbed the key from the air. The car was a small Opel that was newly painted and shiny. It actually belonged to Anders, but because of the companionship Freddy used it almost as much as Anders.

A few minutes later Freddy stopped outside the *Kurbadet Spa*. He got out of the car and went inside.

It was always pleasant to enter the strange atmosphere. The smell of steam, sweat and medicine. But it was the same here as everywhere – it always reminded him of the war. He had gone to the Kurbadet a lot while he was working in Oslo. It had been the only way he thought he could manage to keep somewhat in shape.

The terrible thing was that when he was completely naked, he panicked at the thought of a raid where he risked being caught without being able to defend himself. He remembered the great difficulty it was in getting a pistol hidden, so that he could get hold of it quickly in the event of a raid. In the long run, it became untenable to sit in the sauna naked and just wait for the Gestapo to come because someone had recognised him.

He got hold of a toilet bag. In it he placed a gun with two extra magazines, so that if he was caught he would at least have a chance to defend himself.

He imagined himself shooting his way through the Germans, completely naked. Perhaps he would have his difficulties in getting away. But, there was so many incredible happenings during the war that one could never give up hope until the last spark of life had died out.

A man in a white coat welcomed Freddy. He smiled:

'Good day! I suppose it is to be the usual treatment?'

'Yes!' Freddy said. 'Are there many in there?'

'No, it's not so bad now. It's not like during the war.

I'll never understand how you dared to come at that time with so many Germans here.'

Freddy smiled, he was given a key and a towel.

'No. 14, over there,' said the man.

'I think I'd rather have a room downstairs,' said Freddy.

He got another key and went down a small flight of stairs. Down here it was quiet and still. He opened the door to a small cubicle.

There was a bed, a chair and a small bedside table.

Freddy hung up his jacket, took off his holster, pulled out a drawer in the bedside table and placed his gun inside. The watch and the wallet from the back pocket went the same way. The key fitted the drawer so he locked it.

He undressed quickly, hung up his clothes neatly and took the towel and the key and left the cubicle. He locked the door behind him. At the scales he weighed himself. He had started to put on weight.

He greeted one of the men in white, and saw that another guy with only a towel around his waist was massaging a fat, heavy guy. He made the guy aware of Freddy and said something about him.

Freddy walked past some guys waiting to be dried by the men in white. He saw one of them supporting a young boy who looked like a living corpse.

Poor thing, he must have been one of the polio patients. It must have been desperate conditions for these poor people. They were on long waiting lists to enter the spa home, and had to wait months for a place.

Freddy went into the room that was the sauna. It was blazing hot here. In the sauna there was a small table, two chairs and two benches. Freddy put the towel on one of the benches, took one of the newspapers lying on the table and laid down on top of the towel. It was one of the daily newspapers which he had already read a little.

He took a look at the *Used Cars* ads. There wasn't a single car on which the price was written. He noticed a large advertisement in English stating that the one that had put it there was willing to pay for your ticket to America and back again, either by plane or by boat, if he could buy your car. Freddy had seen the ad several days in a row.

He also took a look at the parts list. It was colossally long. Everything was *Bill Note*. It was probably the biggest fraud that had taken place in Norway.

Freddy himself had been to Northern Norway on a trip in the beginning of 1946, and had seen a bit of what was going on up there. And even then, at that point, there were only the remains left. He remembered that in one of the towns to the north he had been inside a car shop to buy some parts.

Well, they had the parts. The young man had made him aware that they had so much to do that they hardly had time to sleep, as he said. They sent parts down to Oslo continuously, around the clock.

Freddy had asked if they had a lot of parts.

'Well, of course! We bought a whole large shed with parts from floor to ceiling. It was the Germans who had it.'

It had made Freddy a little dizzy:

'You must have earned hundreds of thousands of kroner then?'

'We had to,' said the young man. 'Remember that my father had to pay a hell of a lot of money and a one-off tax.'

Freddy had suddenly understood that the father was the infamous Nazi he had heard about. He had to smile when he thought that there was a certain logic in the company having to hang on and make money. But it had surprised him that such a company could have been bought by the *Directorate for Hostile Property*. But after a while up north, nothing surprised him.

He came to remember *Bardufoss*, (a small town in northern Norway). There he had met one of the finest Norwegians he knew, namely the Commander. This man had done so much good and had always been straightforward and decent in all his dealings.

Now he sat up here in the wasteland like another exile. He who had all of Norway's youth behind him.

It didn't seem to affect his energy and mood. Freddy had been shown around by him. He looked at what this man, despite *the great difficulties*, had managed to create. He looked at the large swimming pool. He listened to his plans. There was to be a sports ground and a soccer field. Here the boys would be allowed to play tennis, and so on.

Up in the air he saw a small plane frolicking.

'It's one of the planes from Little Norway (Norwegian pilot training school in the USA), that we acquired. Some of the land staff are now up and training. I let them have lessons so they can learn to fly too. It raises the interest.'

The small plane landed and took off again, constantly with new students. A small flight school up there in the wasteland.

Otherwise, the airport was a sad sight. There was all the equipment of the Finland Army, neat and tidy. Systematically, in kilometre-long lines, there were all kinds of cannons. All types of armoured personnel carriers were represented. There were anti-aircraft guns in long, long lines. There were ammunition wagons, cannon wagons; lots of rolling material. There were huge mountains of gas masks, helmets, camouflage nets and tarpaulins.

On the whole, it was everything that a modern, well-equipped army could ask for. The Germans had had discipline and order in their matters.

The trusty aviator, who also liked to keep things in order, had tried to keep track of these values, which represented numbers that he could not in his wildest imagination imagine.

'It stands here and rusts,' said the man who had selflessly fought for Norway's cause, day and night since April 9th 1940.

'I have hustled and hustled to get rid of it, but it just stands here and is getting destroyed, all of it.'

Freddy walked over to a heavy cannon. The entire mouth was torn open by an explosion. 'It was the English who had done it. They destroyed all the gunnery by placing explosives in the muzzles of the barrels.'

Freddy looked over the long line of material and shook his head:

'But the chassis and all the carriages, can't they be used?'

'Of course,' said the pilot. 'But it's no use getting them in Oslo to understand any of it. I have tried to get them to use the material, but it's impossible to get them to listen to me.'

Freddy looked at the thousands of rubber tires on all the carts and cannons. It must have had a great value.

'I've had them in Oslo try to transport the metal away, but it seems they think it's too cumbersome, too far, or whatever the hell it is. I don't see how they would be able to transport the iron on the railway once it's finished, when they can't even get rid of all these castings, just waiting to be sent away.'

'But these are only minor things, come with me over here!'

They moved to another place. Here stood the sad remains of what was left of the German Army's motor vehicle fleet. There might have been thousands of cars here. Cars that had themselves been driven into place, row after row, where they had then been taken over by the Norwegian state upon liberation.

Where had they gone? There were still lots of car wrecks here. Without rubber, and everything of value had been picked off. Freddy had seen that sight in so many places around Oslo and would see it again and again later.

He remembered a time when he had been with two appraisers to a German military camp on the outskirts of Oslo. Here it was the Norwegian military who were on guard. The two valuers were to value two cars. They entered a garage. Inside there were two cars jacked up without wheels. The bonnet was missing, everything movable on the car was gone. Even the spark plugs were missing.

The assessors began to take notes, then one said to Freddy:

'You know it's just nonsense to do this kind of valuation?'

He asked the ensign who was there how the hell this car had managed to get into the garage without wheels?

No, the ensign also thought it was a bit strange, but that was how it was.

Freddy remembered when he once heard that a car was to be released from the military, which would be suitable for a workshop van. He investigated it and discovered that it was in a small town on a military camp.

He chose to go down at once, because as the fellow in the directorate with whom he was dealing said:

'Otherwise there won't be a screw left.'

Freddy was still too late. The car had been in perfect order until a couple of days ago.

Now it was a wreck. Everything was ripped off.

- All the thousands of car wrecks that are in the land of Norway, how did they get like this? They were in full order when the Germans capitulated. How is it that the newspaper *Aftenposten* always has long lists containing all kinds of car parts.

- Yes, there is only one explanation: theft - it was the many rotten people that ran the Germans' errands during the war. All the German-workers who thought they were making a national effort when they stole from the buildings or at the workplaces.

-A-ha, maybe they were the thieves?

- The Nazis generally had little chance of staying on speaking terms with the guards. Maybe it was the guards who stole in the first place? Perhaps it was the military - or was it the entire Norwegian people who had sunk into becoming a nation of lazy, unreliable thieves?

- Wasn't it just the same as theft from the Norwegian people that there was still a black market on food-goods? Were the peasants not damned thugs when they continued their black market and took advantage of the hardships of their fellow citizens.

- Where had that spirit gone that had been so praised since the time of the war? Unity! A united Norwegian people who wanted to build up our country.

- Shouldn't we be ashamed today when we think of President Roosevelt who said: 'Look to Norway'. And by that he meant that the Norwegian people were an example for the whole world.

- What happened to the up-bragging of the restoration? Wasn't it all just a huge hoax?

In 1946 Freddy had travelled all the way up to *Kirkenes* (a small Town in northern most Norway), he had seen what the poor people up north had to struggle with. The barracks that were erected became as costly as permanent houses would have been. And they were often set up right on the firewalls. It was all despairing and sad. How would *Finnmark* (the largest county in northern Norway) ever become what it once was? How could Norway even get back on its feet?

Freddy had experienced the types who were on re-construction work up north. Damn! Exactly the same filth that had worked for the Germans. Same mentality. Work as little as possible, earn as much as possible. Drinking them-selves senseless and making noise everywhere.

He had met some Swedish work volunteers who had wanted to help with the rebuilding. They were on their way back to Sweden; they had had enough of it all.

Freddy had been ashamed.

He had also had a strange experience on one of the liners. A fellow, who looked as if he had never experienced soap and water, was walking the corridors and causing trouble. Freddy had asked what he was doing there and the guy had been just rude. Freddy had gone into the saloon where the mate was, and had said there was a guy prowling around the cabins.

The mate had joined him into the passage, had glanced at the guy, and said:

'I can't interfere with him. But you can just throw him out if you want?'

Freddy had gone up to the guy and said he'd better get upstairs if he didn't have anything down there to do.

The guy replied:

'What's the matter with you, you brat!'

Freddy had hit him and then dragged him up the stairs to the deck. Then he had gone down again.

The mate entered the cabin afterwards:

'It was very nice of you to do this Freddy. I've done it myself once, but I can't do it again. He is the boss of the wharf workers, and the result, when I hit him, was that the ship was not unloaded. We have so much trouble up here in the north that we have to be careful. That guy is always drunk and always arguing.'

'But we are powerless.'

This was in 1946. Now it might have become somewhat better - although God knows, Freddy thought.

Now he had begun to sweat in torrents. It was nice to sweat out the alcohol. Liquor was basically a curse to mankind. If everything hadn't been so difficult, and if he only could avoid constantly thinking that a new war was on its way, then he would stop drinking altogether. But as the times were, he thought everything became so trivial. Regardless of whether he drank or not, it slipped quietly into another war without protest, so then one might just as well carry on.

CHAPTER 8

He felt that he had been in the heat long enough so he left the sauna.

There was a small pool with ice-cold water.

By it was a sign saying that you should wash yourself with soap and shower before going into the water. But Freddy loved going completely overheated into the cold water. When he stood still in the water it didn't feel so cold, as long as you didn't move.

His heart pounded inside him. It must have been a hard strain on the heart. He got up. When he moved, he felt how icy the water really was. It was good to get up even though he felt himself getting dizzy. There was a wicker chair there in which he sat down.

After a while he felt better and went back into the water.

He drew in air and let himself slide under the water. He slid along the wall, and in his imagination he was involved in a sabotage job.

He had once participated in a ship sabotage. He had been swimming in the icy harbour water, wearing only a rubber suit.

It had been an extremely demanding job. The risk of

being discovered was high, and the chance of getting away was slim. Still, he thought it was a trifle compared to the *Rat Catching*. It had been wonderful to put the magnetic explosive charge on the ship's side and that was what the wall of water reminded him of now.

Freddy had made it back unseen, but they had made a mistake with the charge that time so it didn't explode.

They had never understood what happened until after the war.

Later, Freddy had not had the opportunity to take part in such a thing. He had been involved in some sabotage jobs on land, and they had been a welcome distraction. It had been something other than the monotonous work that always preceded a *Rat Catch*.

Shadowing and shadowing again. The rats had many dens, and were as much in cover as Freddy himself. Shadowing was deadly, and someone was always caught.

But the device held. It had been a relief when the shot finally fell, after perhaps months of planning and shadowing.

He was now in a hurry to get away, there was hardly time to rest after the bath.

Freddy parked the Opel in Fridtjof Nansen's place. He thought to himself that it was best to call Anders and have him pick up the car. By all accounts, he himself would probably have the fateful blood alcohol level, it would be too risky to drive. It didn't take more than one drink.

The corridor down to the *Telle* restaurant was so covered with mirrors that you had to see yourself, whether you wanted to or not. Freddy straightened his tie a little and saw that his eyes were somewhat bloodshot. It was probably the chlorine and the sauna that had done it.

A waiter was going into the phone box to make a call. He greeted Freddy in recognition:

'They're sat on the right in the small booth you know.'

Freddy thanked him for the information and gave his hat to the lady behind the counter of the cloakroom.

Inside the small restaurant there was a cosy atmosphere. The music from the Hungarian orchestra was perhaps a little too noisy for Freddy's taste, but they played well. The small restaurant had something of that atmosphere a rootless person who has travelled a lot must necessarily inhale once in a while to keep going. As much as Freddy at one time longed for the mountains with their peace and solitude, and the wonderful physical fatigue, that after a day in the mountains - whether hunting or fishing - gave the body, just as much he once in a while needed to feel the strange rush of the wider world. The strange feeling of unsatisfied longing when he saw the somewhat mysterious foreign women who came to this small restaurant.

It probably reminded him unconsciously of the

time when, as a young boy, he sought the great adventure in the large port cities where the boats arrived. He had always tried to get away from the harbour quarter and up to a more cosmopolitan hotel, where he could sit and listen to music - enjoying his drink, and imagine that he was just like everyone else, dancing with the beautiful southern women, instead of being a little sailor with very little money in his pocket.

When Freddy's friends got drunk and went to whorehouses in the South American port cities, Freddy could sit for hours and look at life and envy all the gentlemen in white who so naturally courted the beautiful women which Freddy would do anything to be allowed to be together with. Later in the night, when he walked home to the boat, he had that rare feeling of unsatisfied longing. A faint, warm breeze made the palm trees stand and sway against the tropical sky with all the strange sounds from the nearby jungle and the grasshoppers. He felt the excitement of walking through the harbour quarters which was teeming with ladies offering themselves, with the stench of rotten bananas, urine and poultry; this stark contrast between the white-clad people in the posh hotel, and the vibrant, pulsating wild life that went on in the slums, always set the imagination in motion, and he dreamed to be away from the boat.

He saw himself in spirit as those dressed in white, and the result was that one day he escaped from the boat. He had, after many adventures and much toil, finally experienced being able to sit as one of those dressed in white.

And there would have been no need to sit alone all evening.

Freddy kept standing inside the door and enjoyed the atmosphere in the room. A party of foreigners was sitting at a table. One of the ladies was very beautiful. She was dark and exotic. Freddy let his eyes rest on her for a moment. She looked up and held his eyes in hers for a long time - an insolent long time. At least so long that Freddy had to let his eyes wander.

He went over to the table where Erling was. It was almost a cubicle. Erling was sitting there with three other guys. A waiter was taking orders. Erling stood up and shook Freddy's hand and introduced him to the other three.

Freddy knew the name of one of them and knew he was a bad guy. He was a little too smart. It was said that even though he had played a fairly large role in the home front during the war, he had amassed a lot of assets and wealth.

Erling asked what Freddy wanted to drink. Freddy looked at the watch – it was past three.

'Can I have a whiskey and soda?'

'Erling,' he then said, 'I have to call Anders and ask him to pick up the car.'

Erling nodded and Freddy went to the phone booth.

He looked over at the foreign lady, but she was busy eating.

Anders was not at the workshop but Freddy gave the message to the one who answered the phone. As Freddy passed the foreigners the lady looked up at him and Freddy felt that there was contact. He smiled a little when he approached Erling.

The drinks had just arrived, and the guys were in full discussion. As usual, when Erling offered someone a drink, it became business talk. It was the Directorate for Hostile Property that was discussed. The slightly fat, young fellow whom Freddy only knew by word of mouth, told Freddy that it concerned some huge steam cookers that the Germans had used in their military camps.

'We buy them all,' said Erling, 'and then we sell them to the farmers. They will be fine as pig food cookers.'

'How much do we have to give for them?' asked Fattie, whom Freddy quietly called the unsympathetic guy who had explained the matter to Freddy.

Erling struck out with his hand:

'I will take care of it. That's my business. I know a fellow in the Directorate for Enemy Property. I jumped high the other day when I, with the hat in my hand, visited the Directorate to buy something. I knew there was someone else looking for the same thing and didn't know a soul up there. After waiting some time I was shown in by the tall gentleman with whom I was to confer, I could not believe it - it was Flisa! - amongst all the people on this earth!'

'He sat there with an air of importance and reminded Freddie very little of the old Flisa who was overjoyed to shine his boots when they were in Scotland. But he was fine, and it didn't take long before I had relieved him from his solemn nature. And after we had had several small reunion cups he had been disciplined again, and was basically happy to help me with the coat.'

'I was able to buy what I wanted. Flisa was fine. He was so afraid of being corrupt that I let him pay the whole bill the night we went out, and it was probably more than he could afford on the lousy salaries they have in such ministries.' The others laughed and toasted Flisa.

The fat guy suddenly said to Freddy:

'Freddy, we drop the formalities - call me Odd.'

They toasted it. The other two guys were quieter, but it ended with all of them becoming informal. New drinks were brought automatically.

Odd said that it was strange that there were not more corrupt ministers in the various departments.

'Take for example, the *Directorate for Export and Import Regulation, or the Ministry of Trade,* as it is now called after Brofoss took over. In those departments there are secretaries with the power of little kings. They can actually decide whether a company will go bankrupt or survive!'

'It's terrible to see how older, serious businessmen have to sit for hours in a queue waiting to get in and talk to a guy who will decide whether his shop should be closed or not. Imagine if these guys were corrupt? They have a starvation wage that no human being with their claims can manage to live from day to day. They must be well dressed and usually they had a good education.'

'You know that when such a fellow who sees no opportunity to get a new suit, much less something for his wife, yes - then it is easy for him to write out a small license for a business. That might possibly mean that this business can earn a couple of hundred thousand. Then it is tempting to accept a small *gift of gratitude* from the business of, let's say, NOK 5000.'

'Still, I don't think that will ever happen. Naturally, there have been tendencies for the boys to say yes to a dinner. They have even allowed themselves to be asked to stay abroad to study what is to be imported. And there may have been some wine, girls and song, but cash, no!'

'There must be something about us Norwegians. We don't have the sense of corruption that, for example, the French do. They basically do quite well there. There you ask how much it is, and then you pay.'

'If you put a few thousand on the table of such an underpaid, Norwegian secretary, you can be sure that he will be furious. But if you know someone who knows him, it's much easier to get in to him, and it becomes easier to talk together. Well, that tastes a bit like corruption too, doesn't it?'

'It's quite peculiar. It's typically Norwegian, at least for the Norway of our time, today. It is based on contacts. It happens everywhere, from the housewives queuing at the butcher's, at the greengrocer's, in the factory, car workshops, railway tickets, hotels, I was about to add the tax authorities, but there it's probably no use knowing anyone. I'm damn sure you won't get to heaven if you don't have contacts there.'

One of the silent ones suddenly said something, to Freddy's great surprise:

'Odd is right in what he says. I don't know anyone at the housing office. I have been applying for a flat now since I came home from England in 1945, and I don't think I will get a flat for another 10-15 years. I live in one room with my wife and a little girl aged four.'

'You see, the wife is English. I got married in England during the war,' he explained to Freddy.

He continued:

'The wife is pissed off that we can't get an apartment, and she has said that she will return to England after Christmas if I can't manage to get housing. But I don't give a damn – she has to go. I'm tired of trawling these hellish offices.'

'I was in England three weeks ago,' said Erling. 'It

was expensive as hell there. The whiskey was actually more expensive than here and almost impossible to get hold of. Cigarettes were hard to come by, and a Players pack now cost three shillings and sixpence. Otherwise I think it was fine over there.'

'They're getting back on their feet quickly. You know, they just get on with things. You have to laugh at them, they just carry on, playing Cricket and not giving a damn.'

'There was little warmongering. The newspapers wrote almost nothing about the threat of war and they're building new houses more than they are here. Only the Gods know how they managed it when you consider the colossal damage that had been done. Their housing crisis is settled, and they have even managed to protect what the English say: *My home is my castle!'*

'Cheers to the English,' said Freddy. 'By the way, how goes with the factory?' he asked Erling.

'Well, it strolls and goes,' he said. 'It's the same nonsense with the workers. The rule is to work as little as possible and earn the most. In a way I completely agree with them, but I think that when they are at work they should give a little more. For me, they can earn just as much as they want.'

'I am interested in getting more speed in the production. But the cursed German-worker mentality still remains. It's as if the propaganda we started during the war, go slow, has only begun to work now that we really need to pick up the pace.'

'You heard the story with Willy. Yes, you know, he's crazy when he starts. It's a real shame that we can't have him at the factory. He works as fast as a dozen such German-workers.'

'You should have seen him when we put up the factory. Geez, how Willy worked. Around the clock. He ruled and mastered. I think he knocked down ten, twenty men before the factory stood where it stands.'

'But he got the people going. We were very lucky not to be blocked, but we had a nice little tribe of good working guys, so every time a drunk came in, and Willy lost his temper, there were too many decent guys among the people for there to be a strike.'

'There is hardly anyone who has built as quickly and cheaply as us. We were able to buy a German barracks which we converted into a small factory. By the way, we have now gone into expansion.'

'That desk I bought from you was some damn shit,' said Freddy.

Erling agreed, but he didn't look any more worried about it.

'By the way, we are starting to get more momentum in everything now.'

Freddy saw that Anders had entered the room and

he got up and went over to him with the car key.

'Is there anything new?' he said

'No.'

'Well, I'll be at work early tomorrow.'

Anders disappeared. When Freddy had sat down again the fat young guy who called himself Odd said:

'You have a car paint shop, after all. Do you also take bodywork?'

Freddy said they had too little space and too few people.

'Even if we arranged a workshop for you in a German barracks - do you think you could get enough people?'

Freddy nodded.

'You understand, Freddy,' said Odd. I have a good idea that should make a lot of money. I can get hold of piles of car wrecks. Such cars that have been wrecked due to theft. Those wrecks will probably be classified for scrapping, but I will get that side of the matter fixed. I also know where we can get the missing parts. Not the stolen ones, but new, original parts, that is.'

Freddy lit a smoke. He suddenly felt that he was completely dizzy with hunger. He had forgotten to eat since the meatballs last night, and then he had taken a sauna.

Here we have one of those guys who knows who

is behind the long lists of parts in Aftenposten, he said to himself. Out loud he said he was hungry and had to have something to eat.

Erling got up at once and went to talk to the butler so they could get something good.

The two silent fellows said they had a meeting and had to go. They shook Odd and Freddy's hand and disappeared.

'Poor thing, said Odd suddenly. It must be hell living in one room with an English wife and a small child. I agree with the girl that she is going back to England when conditions are so desperate here.'

'No, surely there wasn't much thanks from a proud fatherland to those of you who were out fighting during the war? I was about to leave once myself when the Germans had cornered me, but thank God it passed, and I continued on the *Home Front* until the very end. I made money like hell from the Germans, but that way it was easier for me to get information about things. I know that a lot of crap has been talked about me in town, but I can tell you that I took far more risks than most of the others who were in the *Home Front*. They tried to arrest me after the war, but I could prove that I had put the money I had earned from the Germans into a special account in a bank.'

'It was my present to the Norwegian state. And then on top of it all I have to pay a damn one-time tax! But let's not talk about taxes. Here comes Erling.'

Freddy smiled as he took a sip of his drink. Gift to the Norwegian state and then one-off tax. It didn't fit together well, as Odd certainly hadn't owned anything before the war.

'Well well, it was always the same lesson. From small smelly German-workers to the big contractors, industrial leaders, businessmen; all had a motive to profit from the Germans. The motive was always the same with small variations. It was either to prevent the Germans from taking over the company, to save Norwegian values, or to obtain information for the Home Front. When you read the minutes you got the impression that every single one of the economic traitors had spat in the coffers of the *Home Front.*

But those fellows weren't exactly poor afterwards. A man who can pay a few hundred thousand in confiscations has probably always managed to hold on to so much that, after all, he came out of the occupation fairly unscathed - at least financially, if not morally. Now look at this Odd, who was always the big man, who paid the bill. He probably had a new American luxury model, plus a large apartment in *Bygdøy Allé* or thereabouts.

No matter how you turn it around, there were many of those who were at home during the war who compared themselves to all the boys who toiled outside for maybe five years. They now stood on the street without education, without means. Young people who might have gone straight from school or started a job in an office.

Today they found out that the guys who had been left sitting at home at the office desk had drawn the longest straw. They had worked their way up to a secure position. They could have charted the course for their lives. They would have been able to get engaged in the normal way, get it published in the newspapers and get married when the equipment and the apartment were in order.

The young airman, who had married his little good mate from the war, went around the settlement offices destitute in order to get a place to live. He may have gone from office to office in despair, discussing the chances of being employed in a company with the young office manager who turned out to be his old schoolmate, and who had not had the courage to join the fight against the Germans.

Perhaps the small, nagging sense of shame in the confident young office manager caused the airman to get the job. But perhaps it worked out exactly the opposite. It could also happen that the same office manager who did not dare to risk anything when it mattered, could condescendingly say to the little aviator:

'You should have listened to me. There was more use for you here at home. But I can tell you it was hell here after you left. I was so unbelievably lucky that I was never caught.'

Well, well.

And then he might have looked up at the wall where there was a beautifully framed participant's medal which showed that he had belonged to *Milorg* (Norwegian military resistance organisation). There may also have hung a picture of himself with a Sten gun and the *Milorg* emblem round his arm.

The young aviator might have taken a couple of benevolent tips and then had to continue his journey. Maybe a little bitter. Perhaps he was thinking of all the many, the despairing many of his comrades, who were now dead, scattered all over Europe. Maybe he was the last of his litter alive?

Perhaps he told himself that now there was no other way out than to start flying again, if he was to manage to provide food for his wife and himself. Perhaps flying again beckoned him. It could be that during the war he had sworn that when peace came, he would not be involved in anything more dangerous than handling a lawnmower on the small lawn in front of the house, which was to become his and his girlfriend's home.

But the young people who were out fighting quickly understood that they had been very young when they made the fateful decision, idealistically - and if necessary - to give their lives for the fatherland. They had forgotten to take into account that older people often forget the ideal they had in their youth. They had also forgotten that the elderly did not always appreciate what the young did, and what was worse, the young had blindly thrown themselves into a fight for what they believed in, and had expected that both old and young would do the same : Fight to end Nazi rule.

The young people had not dreamed that there were actually older people who, in the middle of the war, could think about such trifles as politics. They had no idea there was such a thing as a party book, and they certainly had no idea about it while they sat terrified at the controls of their *Spitfire,* fighting desperately to save their lives, while at the same time doing their duty to shoot down German planes. Perhaps at the same moment that the childhood friend was lying terrified and swimming for his life down in the cabin of a mine-blasted boat, there was another who at the same moment whirled through the air until the parachute unfolded and with a jerk slowed down, so that he slid slowly down towards the dark forest somewhere in occupied Norway, while the young boy gritted his teeth in terror of what might happen in a few seconds when he hit the ground.

At such a moment, perhaps the serious older gentlemen could plan a political propaganda, whether they belonged to the bourgeois parties or the *Workers' Party.* The young people may have heard some rumours about the party book. They may have heard strange stories about relatively reasonable people who could say something as strange as that they were so happy that the *class struggle* could continue abroad. The young active fighter would perhaps shake his head a little and think that the drink was stronger than intended when he saw two Norwegian civilians sitting and talking politics, while the air defence in London played up and the glasses clinked from the detonations of the bombs dropped by the German planes. Perhaps he changed *Churchill's* words: 'We will continue the fight, we will fight from the beaches, from the streets, from the straits' etc., to: 'We will conduct politics from the beaches, from the streets, etc. We will never give up'

Perhaps he laughed hysterically to himself at the thought.

But after the war he had understood that for many people politics was more important than fatherland. Yes, above all! And he had understood that the politicians were to blame for the fact that he had had his entire youth destroyed. That it was the politicians' fault that all the comrades from his litter had met death in their fight for what they believed in. He perhaps also understood that it was party discipline that was to blame for systems such as Communism and Nazism being able to arise. He perhaps also understood that it was because of party politics that a worker could never vote for anything but his own party, although he was ever so unhappy about it. He perhaps realised that the battle going on in political life was much more intense than the one he had participated in with his *Spitfire* plane.

At the time it had been about life; the political struggle was about power. The party that received the most votes would gain the coveted power. They could dictatorially carry out what they wanted, with the power the number of votes gave them.

'Do you sit and dream?'

He suddenly heard Erling's voice.

'I asked if you wanted red wine or dram with your meal?'

Freddy shook his head a little to sort of wake up. 'I really need to get something inside. It's dangerous to drink on an empty stomach.'

'By the way, I was thinking about the war.' It suddenly dropped out of him, much against his will. - 'To hell with thinking about that nonsense,' said Erling. 'When, after all those years in the navy, I was put ashore with just enough kroner to take a night out, someone said to me: - Erling, you've been a fool who has wasted your time in the navy. You would have been a wealthy man today, if you had lived life instead.'

'That was the last time I thought about the war. If there's another war, I'll build barracks for whoever the hell is occupying the country. I've had enough of that idealistic bullshit. Look at Hans, as much as he did during the war. He also received the highest Norwegian war decoration, *the War Cross with Sword*. But do you think it was with great parade, with kisses on the cheek and such?'

'Oh no, it came in the mail and on top of that he had to pay penalty postage! He may have cheated on the postage, but otherwise I know it's true enough.'

'Look at all the guys who first wasted 4-5 years in England. So when they came home, the blue-eyed went into the military. They thought things would speed up.'

'But you saw how it went. Where do you think all the fighter pilots have gone? All together, where do you think the spirit that we had during the war is?'

'To hell with it! What do you think the guys who ended up in Germany have got as a compensation for all the suffering they went through? How do you think their settlement from the Settlement Office is going? How do you think they fare in normal life? How do you think things are going with the survivors of the fallen?'

'Oh no. During the war we didn't spend a penny to invent sunny stories about what it would be like when we got home and had to rebuild the country.'

'Do you remember that it was said so beautifully that it didn't matter if the whole country lay desolate. If we only got the land back, we would build it up again. Well, we got the land back. Just get out on the street and try to find yourself a nice apartment. There has to be enough space for them when you consider that we were prepared to build the country up from the ground.'

'No, - put an end to the war, give a fuck in being blue-eyed to believe in such nonsense as unity and patriotism. It is as my father always says: 'Norway would be a nice country, if there were no Norwegians.'

Erling hit the table so the glasses bounced:

'Let's talk business and make money. There is no one

else but yourself that you can expect to get any help from.'

Erling looked pretty cool when he was angry, and he got angry easily. He had very thick hair that was almost red. Had a lot of freckles and was quite tall and slim, but seemed powerful. His behaviour was sure, but it was as if you could always sense the sailor.

He had basically been a great fit in the navy. Those who had been with him had said that he was completely insane when they went into battle. He had been decorated for a motor torpedo boat raid, where he had been given a chance to particularly distinguish himself.

It was right what Erling said: He never talked about the war. If he ever touched on those things, he always got angry.

Two waiters brought the food. One showed a bottle to Erling, who nodded. The red wine was poured into the glasses. Freddy supplied himself abundantly and began to eat. The small orchestra was playing *Schwarze Augen* - a classic pro German anthem. The conductor walked around the room with his violin from which he practically cried out the tunes. He came over to the table where Freddy was sitting and Erling put a note in his pocket.

Freddy couldn't help it. His thoughts immediately went to a night in Istanbul during the war. He had been among a whole group of Norwegians who travelled around the world to get an opportunity to be beaten to death in the war against the Nazi regime.

It had been a rare all-night-er. The black violinist had been standing with his violin almost down to the ear of one of Freddy's travelling companions. The boy had been very drunk and suffered from homesickness. He had kept getting the violinist to play *Schwarze Augen,* because it reminded him of his girl back home in Norway. All the while he had stuffed money into the violinist's pocket, just as Erling was doing now. The boy had subsequently become an aviator, and was later shot down in his first encounter with the Germans.

Now Erling began to lay out his plans for repairing all the car wrecks they could get hold of. He had arranged a saddle maker, he said, and if Freddy could handle the body work and painting, things would turn around. Erling was to procure American varnish and primer. He was sure to get hold of a German barracks, so Freddy could get a bigger workshop.

Erling presented the plan clearly and matter-of-factly. Freddy had to admit to himself that Erling had a damn good handle on things.

'We are going to earn a hell of a lot on these cars. People are crazy when it comes to old cars, and we can safely let them pay. After all, the buyers are usually those who have taken advantage of us other idiots, who messed with war and the like.'

'I will arrange the business if you and Odd fix the

cash and the parts. Freddy can take care of the purely work-shop-related things, such as having the parts fitted and the appearance fixed.'

'I would like you to understand one thing before we get started. It's an honest business we're going to make. Yes, of course, we are going to make a rough profit and each man gets to cheat the tax as much as he sees fit. It is his own business. But there is no corruption in the company, at least not from my side. I have not yet bribed a secretary in a ministry. I might drink with them, I chat with them and I know them – in other words, I have the contacts.'

'But I never pay for anything. I don't intend to get mixed up in anything that could get me into trouble. How Odd organises himself with regard to spare parts is his business. It doesn't bother me. I mean that whether we buy the parts or not, it is no problem for the fellows who have them to get rid of them, and they are anyhow forever lost for the state.

Erling picked up his fountain pen and began to draw and explain. Freddy watched with interest, when he was suddenly interrupted by a hand being placed on his shoulder. He looked up. It was Harald.

'Can I talk to you Freddy,' he said.

Freddy got up and followed him outside. They sat down in the vestibule.

'It's about Knut, I think he's lost his mind.'

Freddy grabbed Harald by the arm:

'Has he shot anyone?'

'No,' said Harald, 'but that's a risk I fear.'

Freddy took a cigarette and offered one to Harald:

'Tell me from the beginning!'

CHAPTER 9

Harald took a long drag of his cigarette;

'I was in the club a while ago, and it was total chaos. The police had been there to find out if Knut was there, or if anyone knew where he was. We quickly found out what had happened. Do you remember, that when we left he talked about having a girl he could sleep with at night?'

It turned out that this girl had not only been a prostitute, but Knut had become completely besotted by her. She had probably thrown him out when things got bad for him financially. Presumably Knut has nevertheless, as he does when he gets drunk, constantly been trying to force himself on her. They had had violent scenes, and she had threatened to report him to the police.

'Knut had a key to her apartment and likewise to the gate. He had gone straight from us to her. There he got himself into the apartment and then found her with another guy.'

'Oddly enough Knut missed with three shots and the guy got away. It wouldn't surprise me if he's still running for his life,' Harald added with a small grin.

'The neighbours were of course woken up. They had heard the girl screaming, had heard the shots and alerted the police. When they arrived they were greeted by a strange sight: Knut had come stomping down the stairs with the girl slung over his shoulder, with her hands tied behind her back.'

'The police had taken cover when Knut opened fire. He had thrown the girl off and then disappeared across the street. No one has seen him since.'

Freddy stood up:

'Just a moment,' he said, 'I have to give someone a message.'

He told Erling that he had to go. Harald said he had a taxi waiting.

'But what the hell are we going to do?'

Freddy thought it was best to find out what the police knew about the case.

They got out at *no. 19*, Oslo police station, and soon after they were sat with the officer who had the case. So far he knew no more than what Harald had already said:

Thank God Knut had missed. The guy who had been shot at had reported the case, but he had been so terrified that they had actually thought of locking him up for his own sake. He had demanded protection so they had left a constable to look after him.

The questioning of the girl had brought up many strange things. She had said that Knut always had a gun on him, and that it was always next to the bed. He had often seemed disturbed, especially when at night he had suddenly jumped out of bed with a scream and had claimed that someone was in the room to take him.

'You can talk to her yourself,' suggested the officer. 'She's in the next room. She's afraid to go home until we find Knut, which is not surprising.'

Freddy and Harald went into the next room. A woman of about thirty - of a type that reminded him a little of Miriam, although she was much more fragile and smaller - stood up suddenly and looked frightened.

The officer introduced Harald and Freddy, and said that they were two friends of Knut's. Then he went back into his office.

The girl took out her bag and fixed up a powder box with a mirror under the lid.

'Look how I look,' she said and began to powder one eye, which was almost closed after a heavy blow. 'I'm so glad I broke up with him before he went completely crazy, but I should have changed the locks. I'd completely forgotten he had a key.'

Freddy offered her a cigarette and asked if she could tell him about what had happened.

'As I said, I broke up with Knut several days ago. I couldn't stand the strain of being with him. He was kind and pleasant in many ways, but occasionally he acted to me in such a way that I became afraid. And it was crazy with all the guns he was always playing with.'

'He always let me understand that he had to be on guard for one thing or another. I think he was afraid the Nazis would take him or something. The worst was when he didn't dare go home in the evening. Then he was happy to sleep over with me. He often scared the life out of me by jumping up in bed in the middle of the night and screaming out.'

'When I switched on the light, he would come back to himself. He was always ugly to look at when he dreamed like this. He was drenched in sweat, and he looked like the devil himself lying there in bed. When he then woke up, he would always check everywhere to see if anyone was there. Afterwards I had to comfort him to calm him down. Other times he would lie and talk loudly in his sleep. But you can understand it took a toll on me.'

'What did he say then,' Harald wondered.

'Ugh, that was not funny! I often used to wake him up when he had such nightmares. He kept talking about them having to do it; it was an order.'

'Do what?' Freddy asked. The girl looked at him a little strangely. 'You both know Knut. I think he did a lot of strange things during the war.'

'I have understood it to mean that he was one of those who liquidated whistle-blowers. I have heard that he once said in his sleep something like: *She is to be liquidated, it is an order from London!'*

'Ugh, it was so awful. But last evening, or rather last night, he suddenly came in my front door. Thank God it wasn't a particularly compromising situation he found me in, but I had a friend with me, and Knut became absolutely desperate right away.'

'Before we could react he had his gun out and fired. My friend thankfully managed to throw a bottle at him, so he wasn't hit. Knut fired several shots, but my friend managed to get out of the door and down the street in one piece.'

'It was worse for me.'

She suddenly burst into a hysterical cry. Freddy looked at Harald. Harald went to the window and looked out.

The girl continued:

'I think that it must have completely clicked for Knut. He came to me completely bent over, and looked totally wild. I screamed but Knut was completely crazy. He came closer and closer to me, claiming that I had done much damage and that I was responsible for the death of many people. He then commanded me to put my hands in the air!'

'I tried to talk sense into him but it was almost like he was asleep. He said *They* to me and then suddenly hit me so hard I fell to the floor.'

'I think I passed out for a moment. When I came round he was tying me up with one of the curtains which he had torn down. He had also gagged me. I couldn't breathe and was sure my last hour had come as he carried me down the stairs.'

'Thank God the police came at the last minute otherwise I'd probably be dead now.'

Freddy promised that they would try to get hold of Knut, and said that he was sure that Knut had only wanted to scare her. But he heard for himself how foolish that sounded.

Harald and Freddie went back to the policeman.

'It looks terrible,' said Freddy. 'It looks as if Knut has completely lost it. I'm afraid he might do anything now.'

The policeman shrugged:

'Yes, it's hell with the guys like that who got used to having their finger on the trigger during the war. Today, you risk that they forget themselves and think they can fly around with a gun still in their pocket and before you know it they pull the trigger. It's not good. I've spread the word that they must be prepared for him to shoot upon arrest. But such a fellow who was used to hiding in Oslo during the war is not so easy to find. You're his comrades, you must try and help by telling us his cover places.'

'There are many indications that it's his nerves that have clicked. If we can get hold of him and get him locked up so he can't do any more damage we'll be able to save the boy. I'm worried though this will end in blood.'

Freddy promised that he would start a search with his comrades from the Club. And if they found any clues they would call the police right away. He and Harald went out into the street again.

Harald went over to the Club to get all the guys. Freddy tried to get hold of Anders by calling from a phone box, he was lucky and found him. He explained where he was and asked Anders to pick him up. It didn't take long before Anders was there. Freddy explained to him what had happened. Anders apologised that he could not join the search for Knut and explained the reason.

Freddy asked if he could borrow the car. Anders said yes. He asked if Freddy had had too much to drink. Freddy had a thought and called Gerd. A moment later he came out to Anders.

'Gerd said she can drive for me. You can drive me to her.'

Anders did so, gave the car keys to Freddy and left to catch the tram.

Freddy rang the doorbell at Gerd's. He quickly informed her of what had happened and asked if she could drive him. She was ready, they got into the car and began their sad journey into the city to try and save a friend from ruining his own life, either by taking someone else's life or his own.

They tried one *safe house* after another, (places you could stay without being traced). It was always the same. Many were pleasantly surprised to see Freddy again, but they had not seen Knut since liberation. With sadness in their hearts they drove back to Gerd's. She poured tea while Freddy called the Police and the Club. Nothing new. Knut had disappeared from the face of the earth. Gerd buttered a few pieces of bread, they drank tea and ate a little. It was now nearing midnight.

'Poor Knut,' said Gerd. 'I don't think we'll ever see him alive again.'

Freddy had thought the same thing. Gerd poured more tea for Freddy.

'Knut was a Rat Catcher during the war, wasn't he?' Freddy didn't answer but drank his tea.

He then said:

'You have probably got to know a lot after liberation. Tell me Gerd, does everyone at *Viktoria Terrasse* know about those who were involved in rat catching?'

'No,' said Gerd. 'I know a little but not very much. I realised in Knut that there was something that depressed him. He was perhaps the one out of all of you who had the hardest time settling down and starting work again'

A thought suddenly struck Freddy, he stood up immediately.

Gerd looked at him in surprise.

'I have an idea,' said Freddy. 'It's possible it's just bullshit, but I want to try it. Will you join me?'

'Yes!'

CHAPTER 10

Freddy drove the car himself now, he drove quickly out of town. Gerd sat leaning in next to him while he drove. The moon was shining on and off as the clouds kept drifting past and hiding it.

Freddy drove on.

He began to fantasise again. He thought of the many times during the war he drove with his nerves on edge, constantly expecting to be stopped. Was it that strange that Knut had lost his nerves? Wasn't it weirder that it hadn't happened to him before?

Poor Knut. Freddy felt that there was a certain connection between the liquidation of the female informant and the incident in the apartment. It was strange that Knut should carry the girl down after having gagged her. And what he had said to her indicated that there was a connection. That was what had suddenly struck Freddy, and that was why he was driving this way now.

'Poor Knut!'

Freddy let go of the steering wheel with one hand, put his arm around Gerd's shoulder and gave her a small hug. They were approaching the place now.

He slowed down. He thought that if Knut was there

he would maybe shoot. However, Freddy had a feeling that Knut would not do that. He stopped the car and got out. Gerd joined him.

They were now standing on a bridge. Gerd looked at Freddy. He realised that she knew it was the bridge on which the female informant had been beaten and shot.

'You know what I was thinking,' Freddy said. 'But I was wrong it seems.'

He looked down at the river that flowed below them. He could almost imagine Knut lying down there. The moon emerged from a cloud. Gerd thought it was all very creepy and stayed close to Freddy. As she peered over the edge towards the river she kicked something metal.

She picked it up. It was a magazine for a Walther PPK handgun.

It was full. Freddy reached under his jacket and pulled out his gun.

'It's best to be careful, he's been here,' he whispered to Gerd.

They continued towards the bridge. Freddy headed to the place where Knut had found the big rock.

He saw something dark lying or sitting down.

It was a human.

It was Knut.

Freddy carefully walked down to him, his finger still

on the trigger.

'Knut?' he said.

'Yes!' Answered Knut, 'I'm here.'

'We need a big stone for her but all these are too heavy for me to lift. Can you help me?'

'Yes,' said Freddy, 'but come up with me first.'

Knut obediently went up with him. When he saw Gerd he suddenly grabbed his forehead, sat down in the road and began to cry. Freddy bent over him, patted him on the shoulder and at the same time took the gun from him. He checked but did not find a second.

Gerd drove the car forward and they helped him inside. Knut continued to cry for some time then suddenly stopped, they saw that he had fallen asleep.

Gerd drove back to Oslo so Freddy could sit next to Knut. Freddy told Gerd to drive directly to *No. 19*. There he met an officer who told him that the fellow that Freddy had spoken to was asleep at the station and that he should be woken up immediately.

A few minutes later the policeman who had the case, arrived. He looked tired and weary. Freddy explained the matter to him and said that it was probably best to get Knut to the hospital straight away.

The policeman agreed and Freddy handed Knut over to him. Knut was awake now. But he was deathly pale.

He was dirty and had hit his scalp somewhere and blood had run down his face. He was completely lethargic and looked like he was half asleep.

Freddy drove home with Gerd.

During the drive they said nothing. He followed Gerd up to her apartment. She found the liqueur bottle from the night before and poured two glasses, still without saying anything.

'Poor thing,' said Freddy suddenly. 'I was waiting for something to happen to Knut; I almost expected him to go down the drain or something like that. But this is worse than anything. The boy has gone completely mad, and God knows if he will ever recover.'

Gerd unscrewed the lid of a box of cigarettes and took one. Freddy lit it, looking at her. She looked up and looked him straight in the eyes.

Freddy felt his heart begin to pound in his chest. He became short of breath and felt dry in his mouth. It occurred to him that he should take Gerd close to him, kiss her and let nature have what it required. His whole body at this moment longed for Gerd.

At the same time, he was feeling a terrible, almost macabre atmosphere with this matter with Knut. He was in complete turmoil that things had clicked for his mate, and the thought that he might be the next one, bothered him.

His fingers trembled as he held the match. He couldn't fight any more.

With a suppressed sob he suddenly threw away the match, grabbed Gerd by the arm and pulled her close to him. He kissed her passionately and wildly. She bristled at first, then kissed him back. Freddy half carried, half dragged her, still kissing, over to the sofa bed and let himself fall down with her. He stroked her hair, he wanted to say so much to her. He felt he just wanted to start crying.

When he noticed that Gerd began to cry, he regained the use of speech and whispered, softly stroking her hair:

'Don't cry, beloved. I have always loved you.'

The moment he said that, he felt that he truly loved her. That for the first time he sensed a feeling that was not just based on eroticism. He understood that he had always abused the word love by using it inappropriately. He knew that the various love affairs and infatuations he had had, had not been much better than when his old comrades from the sea went to brothels and came aboard and told that they had met the world's most beautiful girl, and that it really was love because the girl had slept with him for half price.

Gerd suddenly threw her arms around his cold neck and pulled his head down to her. She had held out for this kiss - in the same way as someone who has walked in the mountains for a whole day in scorching heat but has not wanted to touch water because they knew it was harmful until the goal was reached.

It suddenly dawned on Freddy that such intense happiness as he was now experiencing would never again befall him. Never!

This moment was worth more than a hundred thousand years in heaven. He wished that time would stand still. Half unconsciously, he wanted all people on this earth to die so that only he and Gerd were left.

'Gerd, beloved Gerd!'

He couldn't find other words for everything he now felt. He felt tears streaming down his cheeks. He tried to think rationally. It struck him that it would be a shame to spoil this special moment of heaven.

As if in a mist far away, he heard Gerd's voice say:

'Be careful!'

He could not and would not take in what she said. His fear of the future, the bad memories. The pressure on his brain eased. But even at this moment his subconscious was working and he sensed he wanted to die in this moment when he had reached the height of happiness.

As he was drifting off into a dreamless sleep he saw Gerd get up and turn off the light. She then lay down next to him. She pulled the blanket over them both. He felt the warmth of her body and hair tickle his nose.

He liked the scent of it.

'Beloved,' he said, 'good night!'

Freddy woke up when Gerd got up and turned the light on. He remained dozing. She went into the kitchen, got water and turned on the stove. He squinted his eyelids a little and saw that she took a towel and a toothbrush and disappeared into the hallway.

Freddy stretched. He wondered for a moment if he should continue to sleep. Then he reached out to a chair beside him and took a cigarette and matches. When his cigarette was lit he took a long drag and thought a little about what had happened.

Now he had come emphatically down to earth again, after a few hours having strolled on rosy clouds.

He was aware that Gerd was a fact he could not get past. He realised that he loved Gerd as much as it was possible to love any human being.

Basically, he had known it all along, from the first day in 1943 when he met her through a resistance contact and she had started working for him as a messenger, a *cut-out*.

He recalled the expressions cut-out and dead drop. The spies used these to secretly distribute information. In *SOE speak* it meant putting papers or photographs in a mailbox, for example a hole in a tree trunk. Or leave it with a secret contact such as a tobacconist where someone else you trusted could later pick it up. This meant that they never knew about each other - this limited the Germans from getting hold of two of the resistance fighters at the same time. This also reduced the knowledge of each other which the Germans would otherwise try to gain by torturing their prisoners.

It had never occurred to him that he was really in love with Gerd. It was as if it would be impossible during the war to kiss Gerd, much less say he loved her.

She had always been such that you almost forgot she was a girl. Always straightforward and even-handed, she took her work, toil and risk, just like any of the boys. She herself had created an atmosphere that made every attempt to treat her as a woman and talk about love almost impossible.

But now it was done and little Gerd was a woman whom he loved and who reciprocated his feelings.

He suddenly thought of Miriam and felt a nasty, nervous, sucking feeling in his stomach. Poor Miriam – perhaps she had been waiting for him again all night?

Freddy got a bad taste in his mouth and wished he had a toothbrush. It suddenly hit him that he still had the toothbrush in his inside pocket, from the morning. My God, wasn't that long ago? He thought the last 24 hours had been as long as a bad winter. There had certainly been little sleep, he felt completely exhausted. Freddy jumped out onto the floor and got dressed.

When Gerd came back in he was fully dressed. Gerd looked fresh, freshly washed and well-slept.

A strange feeling of shyness suddenly came over Freddy.

'Good morning Gerd,' he said, 'slept good?'

He wanted to hug her and kiss her, but he would have liked to have brushed his teeth first. Her fresh appearance and freshly brushed, shiny, white teeth gave him the feeling that to kiss her now, before he got rid of the bad taste in his mouth, would be like emptying a rubbish bin onto freshly fallen snow outside a mountain cabin, on the first day of Easter!'

'Here's a towel and soap,' said Gerd.

'I happen to have a toothbrush with me,' said Freddy.

Gerd handed him some toothpaste:

'Unfortunately, I don't have a shaving kit.'

Freddy went out into the hall and found the bathroom according to Gerd's description. He brushed his teeth, gargled and then washed himself. He wet his comb and let it slide through his hair. When he came in, Gerd had set the table and was pouring the coffee.

Freddy put down the towel, soap, toothbrush and toothpaste and went over to Gerd. He put his hands on her shoulders and turned her around to face him. He then put his arms around her and kissed her. Gerd stretched her arms up around his neck and kissed him back passionately.

The kiss was wonderfully fresh. It somehow reminded Freddy of when you sink your teeth into a big, juicy sour apple.

'Gerd,' he said. 'You don't regret it?'

Gerd laughed.

'Freddy, I've been waiting for this for five years!'

'You little devil!' Freddy said.

He sat down at the table and Gerd poured the coffee. She constantly had to reach across the table to grab Freddy. It suddenly struck him that although he was not the first man in Gerd's life, he was the first she had truly loved.

It was really strange. Freddy had been in love and captivated by many women but had soon discovered that after the initial glow, it was not enough anymore. For the first time in his life Freddy felt that he really loved someone - he had no doubt that what he felt for Gerd was something completely different from what he had felt before.

This was what hid behind the so often misused word *Love*. Perhaps more often than most people, Freddy had experienced what he thought was love, but which was never the real thing.

In the tropical night he had been in love with a small black-haired señorita. He had *loved* a clever American, who always first, pulled out a handkerchief and wiped off her lipstick before she kissed him.

He also remembered a wonderful night in the South American jungle with a young local girl, who almost magically in an instant, with the help of the magical atmosphere of the jungle, the heat, and Freddy's strong young body that rose against her, had managed to make him imagine that the only sensible thing for him to do was to settle down with the locals and live their life!

He recalled a woman in London who he thought was the greatest adventure of his life and had so nearly ended in marriage.

And now he was married to Miriam and that marriage was basically no more than what he had deserved. Perhaps now came the hangover he had always been waiting for. He had thought it would come in the form of a bullet from a fanatical Nazi. He had always felt that he had gotten too lucky through the war. The fact that he had come out of the five years of horror safe and alive had always seemed like a miracle to him.

There had to be a hangover, he said to himself. Something wrong had to happen and now it would.

'Gerd,' he said, 'I have behaved like a pig towards you.'

He took her hand:

'But I would like you to understand that despite the fact that I am married and have loved women before you, I have never known what love was. This is no passing adventure. We are made for each other. You must feel the same as me and nothing will stop me. Miriam will surely give me a divorce at once.'

Gerd looked down at the table where she was rolling a ball of the bread.

'Freddy, we were so careless last night. I'm terrified inside when I think about it, but there was nothing on this earth I wanted more, and now it's happened. If I get pregnant I don't want you to worry about it. I'm used to standing on my own two feet.

Freddy said nothing. He looked at Gerd. She was still looking down. Big tears began to roll down from her eyes, they followed her nose all the way down to the tip and there they hung like pearls before dropping onto the table. Freddy was not wearing a handkerchief as usual. He stood up and put his arms around her shoulder.

Gerd burst into tears and laid her head onto him:

'Oh Freddy, I'm so stupid, but I'm so scared.'

'Little darling, everything will be good. Don't cry my darling.'

He gently picked her up in his arms and carried her over to the sofa. Here he stayed and stroked her hair.

He let his mind wander again. What if he ran away from everything and took Gerd with him? He could probably collect a few thousand Kroner if he went into business with Erling. He would always get some money out of his share in the workshop.

During the war Freddy had become acquainted with a ship owner who had told him that he would always be able to count on a free trip on one of his boats anywhere in the world. He suddenly had a wild urge.

He said to Gerd:

'Beloved, I know what we should do! Let's not give a damn about all the shit here at home, let's head out and travel! We go either to Columbia or Venezuela. I can take a job in a gold mine in Columbia or in the oil company in Venezuela. They pay staggering wages, and within a few years we will have saved up so much that we can go to Chile and buy a farm. You see I'm going to make big US dollars, and in Chile they have little lousy Chilean pesos which there are many to every dollar!'

Freddy was excited with the idea, and brought Gerd along in his enthusiasm by telling her how wonderful it was in the tropics. He tried to describe a night in the jungle when he was paddling down a river in a canoe. He wanted Gerd to sense the atmosphere of slipping under the dense primeval forest that overhung the rivers. The mystery that hid behind the dense wall that was the primeval forest. He tried to bring alive for her all the strange sounds which waved back and forth in the night time of the forest.

He said that the moon is never so big as when it shines on the river on such a warm tropical night, which flows like a long soft country road of shimmering silver. He tried to evoke the unique atmosphere of the southern cities; the music, the drums, the smell of people and fruit. He let himself recall vividly the sticky feeling of always having pineapple juice on his fingers, the sweating heat and the cold drinks.

Freddy dreamed back to the hot life of the jungle. This strange atmosphere of eroticism and mystery.

In the back of his mind he knew that he purposely omitted to tell Gerd about the stench of the water in the dirty rivers. The terrible smell of rotten fish, excrement and rubbish from the street all floated together. He did not tell about all the mosquitoes and about the fear of snakes and scorpions. He also did not tell about the many nights when he tossed back and forth on the field bed without being able to sleep because of the heat. He mentioned nothing about fever and illness.

He forgot how often he had lain moaning in the heat and fantasised about being surrounded by snow sitting by a mountain spring with crystal-clear fresh water. He only told Gerd what he felt at the moment and he tried to be honest.

'When I'm in the jungle, you can live in the city. There you have all the comforts.'

Gerd was, with or against her will, carried away by his zeal. But suddenly she remembered Miriam.

'What about your ....?'

She changed it to Miriam. For some inexplicable reason, she refused to say *your wife*.

Freddy got up, lit a cigarette and started pacing the floor.

'I would like to try to explain something to you about Miriam,' he said, 'but it is difficult for me to know where to begin. I think I'll start with childhood, although it's all a bit messy for me.'

'I don't know if I had a bad or good time when I was little. Most people would probably say that I had a poor upbringing but such people might not understand what it meant for a small boy, without too much trouble to be able to skip school and wander the woods and fantasise about Indians, bears and other strange things.'

'I think I was poorly equipped with clothes, and my home was probably a terrible mess where nothing was in order.'

'My father had been a sailor and all sorts of weird things, as far as I could tell. Now he had settled on land and ran some kind of mechanical workshop or something like that. I have never seen my mother. Father never spoke of her. I am not sure if she had run off with another man.'

'My father was all right in many ways. I think he

was good at his work, but as I got older, more and more often, he packed his rucksack and went into the woods and the trips became longer and longer.'

'We had a girl who looked after us for several years. I think she was my father's mistress at the same time. Namely, I experienced some scenes between the two that indicated that it was not servant and employer who were talking to each other. I also think that she always insisted that father marry her.'

'But he never married. He was basically kind to me in every way. We always had a good time together when we were out in the woods. He let me shoot from a very young age. We were always out shooting. In the hunting season we went for grouse and big game and in the spring there was roost migration and game hunting. If it was outside hunting season we shot crows and anything else that was available.'

'We lived very rurally in a kind of cabin. Right outside the door we set up a shooting range, and there we shot with a small calibre rifle. My father was crazy for hunting and skipped work when he could to go to the forest.'

'As I grew older his trips became longer and longer and one day when I was about 14 years old he disappeared for good.'

'I have never seen him since. The woman who looked after the house for us and I had become accustomed to his long trips that could stretch over weeks. In the end, we did not react until several weeks had passed.'

'I actually have no idea what was done then. I assume he was wanted.'

'I had finally struggled through primary school and was drifting around trying to earn some money by helping the grocer and such.'

'Then one day I saw in a newspaper that there were some flower arrangements that had been placed in a kind of basket. I went straight home and climbed up in one of the huge birch trees that stood outside the house. Here I cut down a branch. I started to try my hand and made a small nest you may have seen so often being used for tulips, so-called bird's nests. I made some samples and went into a flower shop with them. They were interested so I went home and started fabricating.'

'My *factory* was quite simple and the machinery even simpler. It consisted of a saw bench, a heavy saw, hammer, steel wire, a small pin, and then I sharpened a large bread knife and made a small wooden block. Finally, I made a mark on the bench and nailed a small wooden block to it.'

'This little mechanism was the real magic. Long dart twigs were placed on the table and pushed forward to the stop block, and then I put the knife where the mark was. With a blow of the hammer, I cut the long, straight branches, up into equally long lengths for the bird's nests. Then I got hold of a birch trunk that was straight and nice and had the right thickness. I put it on the saw bench and cut straight slices that became the bottoms for the nests. The next thing was to collect old milk cans, cut off the lids and insert them into the nests.'

'To get it technically correct,' Freddy added with a smile, 'I put four legs on the disc I had cut from the birch trunk, after which I put a ring on a flexible willow twig on top. The birch branch was then twisted on the outside and fixed with steel wire. Thus the nest was finished, and then it was just a matter of selling it.'

'My little *factory* went well. I kept coming up with small improvements and found a girl who eventually took over the sales. I think we got the staggering sum of 60 øre per item, roughly the cost of an ice cream. It wasn't much when you consider that I had to climb between heaven and earth in those huge Birch trees.'

'I'm very serious about this Gerd, so you understand that I had to learn to stand on my own two feet early on.'

'My childhood was messy, but I think I was, in a way, happy. I had a good time with my mates; they thought it was grand that I had my own gun and fishing rod, and that I was big and strong for my age.'

'I think I was probably more lazy than stupid at school too. Later, after I got older, it wasn't always fun not having more schooling than I had. I think that I have always had a sense of making money, and after my small factory business, I started selling flowers.'

'I found out that it was much easier to sell the small nests finished with blue-veins in the spring. Later I found out that I could buy flowers and put them together and from there it was a short step to just selling flowers.'

'There is a small clique of people who hang around the market and buy up bunches of flowers from the gardeners. They then sell these flowers on the street after the market closes.'

'You've probably seen them standing there with their baskets. They often buy the flowers for a lick and nothing and make a good profit from the sale. Perhaps they cheat a little - like buying a tulip with *water break,* as it is called in the business. There are tulips that break in the middle. They can basically only be used as wreath decorations, but we were specialists in stiffening them up by putting a steel wire through the stem. It was a bit comical when arranging perhaps fifty bundles of such broken tulips. If the sale went brilliantly, afterwards the street could be strewn with half tulips that the ladies had lost from their bouquets. But just as proud, they wandered on with a firm grip around a bundle of tulip stems, while the steel wires poked out of the paper.'

'This was my first step on the business path.'

'It perhaps struck me that it was easiest to get the biggest profit if you were dishonest, but I soon found out that you could make money even if you were honest. Admittedly, I had to struggle more. I started door-to-door with flowers and soon worked up a nice little circle of customers who always knew I had fresh, first-class flowers.'

'It was tough to get up and down the stairs. But it was nice every day to be able to count the profits. It happened, when it was a bad day, that I skipped school and went to the forest again. On such days I always hoped that my father would return.'

'My way of life hadn't changed much. I lived alone at home with the girl. I could never have put up with her, but she was probably responsible for me, she thought, and I at least gave her most of what I had earned.'

'The time came when I started to take an interest in the opposite sex. I became terribly shy when I bumped into a swarm of girls on the street where I came by struggling with a heavy basket on my arm. I wanted to get away from it all, to try and become something.'

'One day I applied for hire on a boat and got the job as a greaser in the machine room. It was terrible to tell my girl that I was going to sea. There was crying and gnashing of teeth, but I left, and after that I heard nothing from her.

'I've suffered a lot in my life Gerd. I have gone through the most incredible things, but have always managed to get back on my feet as a *white* man.'

Freddy stopped a little when he heard himself call himself *white*.

'I'm not against coloured people Gerd - that's not

what I mean. But it's a stupid old expression from narrow-minded people that has stuck around. Of course, a *white* man is no more honest or better than those of another colour. Not at all.'

'But don't let me stop there.'

'I thought that the life I had led for so many years would make me well suited for rat catching. But there I was wrong. I have seen people killed during fights, I have seen others crushed while working in the mines. I have experienced the hell of an earthquake in Chile. Once I accidentally ended up in an asylum in Havana and when I woke up drunk I saw things that cannot be described.'

'For three days I fought day and night with *naked animals* who wallowed in their own excrement in the large cage I was locked in.'

'But I kept my cool, and came out again without it having made any major impression on me, I think. At least not then. But the rat catching taught me what none of the other experiences had been able to.'

'When liberation came I was a complete wreck. I was possibly physically too strong to have a real breakdown, but I was going straight to the dogs. I drank like crazy day and night.'

'Then I met Miriam. The first time I slept with her it was like medicine for my nerves. I calmed down. I got to sleep. Little by little I got back to normal.'

'I developed a crush for her and then, one day, we were married.'

'I don't want you to think that I'm standing here trying to excuse myself. But ever since my childhood I have longed for warmth and love. I have always longed for it, and it has often cost me trouble. With Miriam, there was so much that came into play. The rat catching and the last part of the war, with the intense pressures, destroyed the nervous system completely. And my longing to have a home of my own was more intense than ever. I thought for a time Miriam could give me what I longed for.'

'You have met her, I don't need to explain to you why I believe that I must have been crazy when I associated Miriam with a small home with children and what should be in a home, namely harmony.'

Freddy stopped his walk and lit another cigarette.

'What do you want to do?' said Gerd.

'You understand,' she added quickly, 'I understand the whole thing so well from your side but you can't simply draw a line over Miriam. You are married to her.'

Spontaneously Freddy said:

'Will you marry me, Gerd, when I'm a free man?'

Gerd got up from the sofa and came to him, put her arms around his neck, stretched on tiptoe and kissed him.

'That's my answer,' she said, 'I love you, and I can't

live without you. I will gladly accompany you to South America, even if you don't get a divorce.'

'Life is so short beloved. We have no time to lose. We've already wasted enough time. I am dying to create for you the home you have never had. It basically means nothing to us whether one or another priest says a few words or not. I have lost all respect for priests since I heard a priest, who is my uncle - a different one than when he's with a bottle - say that he was annoyed that people always died in the spring, because he said he had to waste time in the cemetery.'

'Now that uncle of mine is a keen farmer at the same time as he is a priest, and when he stands in the pulpit it is right that he mixes some carrots and potatoes in among all the godly talk. It comes from him standing and thinking about the farm's operations.'

'You know that whether such a fellow gives us his blessing or not, it's completely indifferent to me. I'm sure that the good Lord will think that it's absolutely right that we live together when we love each other.'

'But you have to clean things up somehow with Miriam.'

'I'm going right now,' said Freddy, 'It's better to jump into it than crawl.'

He kissed Gerd and left.

CHAPTER 11

When he was well down the street he began to dread the meeting with Miriam. Damn it too, that he had got messed up in this nonsense; he felt sorry for her now. He wondered how he was going to explain everything to her. She was probably going to have a hysterical fit.

'Fuck!'

He looked at the clock. It was a quarter past seven. He automatically started to wind it up, he hadn't done that last night. Perhaps it was best to pass by the workshop first. Basically, he should have informed Harald as well - he had completely forgotten that. Maybe they were still looking for Knut, poor Knut. He had completely forgotten about him, but perhaps that was not so strange.

At the workshop he found Anders in full action with a spray gun. He was spraying a small Mercedes blue.

'Anders, come into the office, we've found Knut,' said Freddy.

He told the whole story to Anders.

'So he must obviously have gone crazy. The whole thing must have been set upside down around in him, and then he mixed up the liquidation of the girl and the women who gave him the resignation.'

'It may have been the shock of discovering her with another man, which could have been the final straw. It's God's luck that he didn't kill anyone.'

'Now it's going to be a hell of a row. They'll probably investigate how it is that Knut has a weapon. He didn't have a permit to carry one.'

'I think it's crazy to fly around with a gun,' Anders said. 'It can so damn easily become a fuss. Just think of Helge! You remember he got five years. If he didn't have a gun he would have escaped with a small charge for knocking out teeth and such.' Freddy remembered the story very well. Helge was one of the guys who had had to escape from Norway during the war. He was happily married and had a small child whom he loved more than anything on earth. He would always occasionally show off photographs of both his wife and the child.'

Long before the war was over he was sent to work in Northern Norway. There he had been injured during a skirmish with the Germans and had only come to Oslo after liberation. Now it turned out that his wife had been living with another man, and she was giving a small baby a bottle when Helge came stomping through the door beaming with joy.

The result was the usual, Helge went straight to drunkenness. For a long time he was ripe for the mental hospital but gradually got back on his feet.

Then one day it hit. He had found out which man it

was that had ruined his marriage and unfortunately Helge had a gun on him when he went to talk with him. Calmly and composedly, he had put eight bullets in the guy and then reported himself. In court he had refused to speak, he had only sat with a mocking grin and he had managed to get the judge to accept him. He had been given five years and had accepted the sentence immediately.

Freddy agreed with Anders, maybe Helge would have gained just as much from beating him up, but the fact was, he had a gun on him.

'Do you think Knut will be OK again,' asked Anders.

'It's not easy to comment on that,' said Freddy, 'there is so much that comes into play. I think that if he goes to a nerve clinic and calms down it shouldn't be that difficult to get him back on track.'

'I can understand that *rat catching* could make anyone and everyone crazy,' said Anders. 'It's one thing to shoot a man down in the street without further ado, it must be another thing to interrogate him first, and then go for a drive knowing that you'll soon have to take the life of a human being in the same way as you slaughter a pig. And yet people are talking about war again.'

'No, damn it Freddy, if there's a war I'll run away. They won't be able to trick me into that bullshit again. Admittedly, I didn't get close enough to someone's life that I had to stab them with a knife and such.'

'But I don't easily forget when I was in the canal keeping my best friend afloat in a dingy, he was screaming because his whole stomach had been torn open by a splinter grenade. It's amazing what a person can endure before dying. You can imagine what it means to constantly have salt water gushing into you, when you spasmodically try to hold your intestines inside your stomach with your hands.'

'No, that experience was more than enough for me. I can hear the screams again at any moment. If I want to see blood or hear screams, I can go out into the street and slap a guy in the face, that's enough for me. Then I either get a beating or give a beating.'

The phone rang. Freddy took it.

'Yes, thank God,' Anders heard him say. 'It was Gerd and I, we found him under the bridge where he had liquidated that girl during the war. He's gone completely crazy.'

'OK, I'll wait for you here.'

He hung up.

'It was Harald, he'll be here right away. I think he is totally depressed. It's quite strange. I didn't think he was particularly enthusiastic about Knut. After all, Knut was usually very quarrelsome and irritable.'

'You know it's very strange when something as awful as this happens to a friend. You can soon easily forget small and trivial things. I've always after liberation, been a little envious of you guys who continued in the Linge Company.

I think most of us were, the ones who went into the Navy and the other branches of the forces. We've heard so much about what you accomplished and the life you led during the occupation.'

'I understand now that it was not a walk in the park.'

'Well,' he said thoughtfully.

It became quiet for a little while.

'I'll have to continue with the spraying,' Anders said, and went out.

Freddy picked up a newspaper that Anders had brought with him. It was a morning paper. He quickly flipped through and thank God there was nothing about Knut. Then he looked at the headlines. That was the usual. There was supposed to be a meeting in Moscow again. The war in Palestine continued despite Count Bernadotte and the *United Nations.*

It seemed to be hell in France. The government had resigned and it was apparently difficult to form a new one.

The whole paper was permeated with unrest. It was as if there was a common thread from the first page to the last. An undertone that kept repeating the same thing over and over again: There will be war!

Everything we went through all these years, Freddy thought. Everything that young people have sacrificed in their young lives, their education, their zest for life, perhaps their agility. Hundreds of thousands have become blind, hundreds of thousands are completely crippled, others partially. Thousands of promising sportsmen today sit with wooden legs and watch their mates compete on the sports field. Hundreds of thousands of young men around the world are today locked up in mental hospitals, reliving every minute of the hell they went through.

Maybe everything has been in vain.

Think of Knut who could never forget the horrible scene on the bridge. Was it strange that he went crazy when he discovers that maybe it was all in vain, and that we have to go through it all again, maybe even worse. With fanatical fifth columnists who imagine that they are fighting for what is right and correct.

Perhaps we will experience seeing huge posters hung everywhere on streets and straits. *Norway's salvation goes through the Communist Party.* Perhaps we would see a picture of Stalin on Karl Johan with flowers in front, and an inscription below: *You don't know him.*

Then it would be the same all over again. Confiscation of the radios that people had so painstakingly reacquired. And perhaps the workers who had just begun to pick up the pace again would listen to slogans that they should start sabotaging again and work slowly. The underground secret newspapers would start again. Sabotage would flourish again. The houses that had been built after so much effort would probably soon lie as piles of rubble. The schools would be closed. The newly healthy youth who had grown up would have had their studies interrupted. We who are young, yet ancient, would have to go to a concentration camp, or go underground again if we had been part of an underground movement.

The Gods must know how it will go with the Nazis. Those who fought against the *Bolsheviks* as they said, would perhaps be taken from Ilebu (prison) and sent to Siberia. Perhaps if they were torturers they would be promoted to instructors in torture or given tasks in the concentration camp administration if Norway's new masters did not have enough specialists.

For the ordinary man in the street it would probably be a bit of a stretch. He is not particularly fat today but it could always get worse. His tired nervous system from the five long years would have a hard time coping with the same thing again.

This time with the ever-looming fear of the atomic bomb. It's one thing to run to the shelter like during the war. Then the little man in the street could always take comfort in the fact that when the air-raid alarm went off, it was either saboteurs who were dropped, or if there were bombs, it was always the Germans.

If there is another war, he will have Hiroshima fresh in his memory. He will remember pictures from the newspapers, from films, from books. He wants to know when the air raid warning goes off that if a nuclear bomb is dropped, then it's all over. The Russians will almost certainly invade

Europe. It will be like the big well-known steam road roller rolling along. All resistance will be suppressed. The small forces which the American and the English have in Europe will not be regarded as any opposition.

What about Norway? Won't our resistance be like a hedgehog that confidently relies on its spikes, curls up and calmly awaits the huge steamroller that comes rolling closer and closer. Who will even notice that it crushes the hedgehog into a small mark on the asphalt.

Freddy knew better than most that during the war all the Nazis were marked, put on lists and mapped. When peace came, they were caught within a few hours.

Freddy was convinced that there were people in our country today who were working to become fifth colonists when the time was right. They probably put exact name after name on their lists. District by district throughout the country of Norway was mapped.

If the enemy came into the country again it would hardly take long to place everyone who could possibly offer resistance behind the barbed wire, or shoot them.

The army that would move in would not be any ordinary Sunday school on the march. They had traditions built on violence and terror. After all, the entire Nazi system was an imitation of the Russian Gestapo, an imitation of the *GPU*. Naturally one had to admit that the Germans were not bad apprentices and in certain things they could actually teach the master a little.

But it would only make the situation worse when the master was now fully trained.

CHAPTER 12

Freddy was pulled out of his thoughts by Harald standing in the doorway. Freddy explained to him what had happened and where he had found Knut.

'We have to do something for Knut right away,' said Harald, 'I think we should drive down to *Fruen* and talk to her.'

Freddy took the phone book and looked for her name. He found it and called. As he waited for an answer he thought of her, they always called her the *Lady*. She belonged to one of the finest families in Norway and during the war had been of absolutely invaluable help to a large part of the home front. She mediated contact both with the Danish aid and the large industrialists who were willing to spit in the coffers financially. She had contacts everywhere and had constantly tried to help the boys whom she called *the guys from England,* to work. Also those who needed a loan to start something.

Fruen answered the phone. Freddy explained that something had happened and asked if he and Harald could come and see her.

A while later they were sat with Fruen.

She was very serious. She said that she knew little about Knut; she had never really liked him - there was something about him that did not please her. But as she said, one had to think about his efforts during the war and she was going to help him as much as she could.

She thought they had to get him examined by a psychiatrist first. They had to find out if Knut really was insane or if he had had a breakdown.

Was there a nervous breakdown that was to blame for it all and was there a possibility that she could arrange it so that he could be sent on a ship on a several-month recreational trip. She had arranged it this way for several people who had nervous breakdowns after the war.

'It is now a well-known fact,' she said, 'that you do not go through five years of constant nerve pressure without sooner or later having a reaction.' Such a trip by ship usually had a very fortunate effect.

The Norwegian shipowners were quite unique in this way. There was never no in their mouths. They thought it was terrible that our boys should go to the dogs, as thanks from the fatherland for risking so much.

Fruen called a very well-known neurologist. Freddy understood that it was a girl who answered the phone and she did not want to disturb the doctor.

Fruen said it was important and gave her name. A moment later, Freddy realised that she was now talking to the doctor. She hung up the phone for a moment and asked Freddy if he had a car with him.

Then she said into the phone:

'We'll be there in ten minutes.'

She turned to Freddy and Harald.

'We could come right away,' she said. 'You have to wait a bit and I will be ready. I'm only going to throw on a dress.' She was in her morning dress and now disappeared inside to change. Freddy offered Harald a cigarette:

'You basically didn't have much to do with her during the war, Harald?'

'No,' said Harald, 'not until the end. I was about to leave when she was caught. I waded right into the Gestapo, you understand. I must have had a slight black-out, you know the kind you get when you've kept things going for too long here at home. I actually forgot to call before I went to see her and didn't come to myself until I was standing there with Gestapo police everywhere.'

'Then she had just been taken. I pulled out my gun at once and it all went a little too quickly for the Gestapo. Before they came to their senses I had already disappeared.'

'It probably worsened the matter considerably for her. But thank God it was just before the liberation so the Gestapo was probably interested in keeping a low profile as much as possible or if it was the case that they were so bogged down in work that they couldn't handle all the cases. I don't know.'

'At least Fruen got out of it alive.'

'Yes, she was brilliant during the war,' said Freddy, 'and yes she is good to have now.'

Fruen was now ready so they drove. The doctor lived in a large villa and the maid showed them straight into a cosy room where there was a glowing stove. Freddy knew the doctor and introduced Harald to him.

He began to explain the story to the doctor. The doctor interrupted him:

'I'm not much of a morning person so I haven't eaten breakfast yet, I've told the maid that there will be breakfast for all of us.'

All three had eaten. Freddy kindly replied;

'A cup of coffee would be nice,' he said for all three.

The Doctor began to eat, the other three were poured coffee and Freddy continued with the story but was interrupted by the Doctor.

'I must know absolutely everything. If you think that there is something that all of us here at the table should not hear then we can talk about it in private afterwards.'

Freddy thought about it a bit. No, Harald knew what had happened, and Fruen was known for being able to keep her mouth shut.

'I will tell you everything,' he said.

He began by telling what he knew about Knut's childhood, about his life in England, and how nervous

Knut had been about the skydiving. How he felt he had to throw up when he got scared.

The boys had been teasing him about skydiving for a long time before he finally got to try his first jump. When Knut finally stood at the airport with the parachute on his back waiting to get into the plane, the accident had happened, the party that jumped in front of them had been unlucky with a man.

The parachute had not deployed properly. Like a rock with a long string trailing behind it, the boy came hurtling towards the earth. The parachute had been hanging like a sausage after him. Nearer and nearer to the earth he had come whirling.

They could see him more and more clearly. The boy had been conscious until the last moment but had been completely helpless.

Nothing could save him. He had hit the ground right in front of them with a terrible smacking sound.

Knut had only turned a little and thrown up as he stood in line waiting to enter the plane. They then entered the plane and took their seats. A small group of young Norwegian boys who fought for what they believed in.

Some became deathly ill with horror after what had happened. Trembling with terror that one of their comrades now lay crushed on the ground.

Actually, many of the boys were hoping the whole

thing would be called off.

It was war, and war demanded its victims. The exercises had to go on.

The aircraft took off and climbed to jump height. It was turbulent and the plane shook like a small piece of paper in a storm.

After a while they came across the drop site. They had to circle a bit before it was clear on the ground. They had looked at each other as they sat with clenched teeth, green in the face, but willing to sacrifice everything.

The first man readied himself.

Then the light turned red. They had ended up in a large cloud of fog.

The plane had to circle again and the red light was extinguished.

The red light came on again, and then green. Everyone held their breath and stared at the first man. Would he be able to jump?

He sat completely stiff, white in the face. Suddenly he was no longer there.

The plane circled again. The next one sat chalk white in the face with his legs down in the hole and waited.

Red light: *Action station:* Green light: 'go!' and he vanished into thin air. Out into nowhere. Perhaps he owned nothing but his own young life. Now he whirled down through the air with his hands convulsively clutching the hem of his trousers as he had learned. Would the parachute deploy? Oh dear God let it unfold! Perhaps he envisioned the terrible image of his comrade coming whirling straight down towards the earth. Maybe inside he heard the terrible crash as the boy was smashed to the ground. Then finally came the shock. He looked up. The parachute had opened.

The plane circled. Boy after boy jumped.

Then it was Knut's turn. Knut had been envious of each and every boy who had gotten out through the hole. He had thought:

Now it's over, now they're on the ground.

Finally, Knut sat with his legs down in the hole. He didn't dare look down. He concentrated as hard as he could, he had to get out through the hole, there was no going back.

A red light came on. He waited, then word came that he should NOT jump.

Half swooning he pulled his legs up. The hatch was closed and a while later the plane landed.

The fog had completely closed in and they had no choice.

It had been particularly bad for Knut. He had been envious of his comrades who had made it through the first jump.

It turned out that the first man had broken his femur. The instructors had explained that it was his own fault because he had not done as he had been taught.

The parachute belonging to the one who had been killed was examined. There was no particular fault but it had not unfolded properly. He was a small fellow with curly fair hair whom they called *Himmelspretten* (the sky bouncer) presumably because he was so good at jumping on skis. For the first time they used his real name.

After the accident no one could call him Himmelspretten anymore.

Knut had probably had a bad night where he just lay there and tossed back and forth and couldn't sleep at the thought of parachuting. Later he eventually got through the jump like everyone else. But it had always challenged him physically.

Later when on work duties he had been unusually unlucky. First he had to wait a whole week at the airport for nothing then three planes left in one night. The plane Knut had been in had circled the drop-off site in Norway but had not been able to locate itself due to bad visibility.

Knut had, after sitting with his nerves on edge for four hours, finally had his legs out of the hole in the plane just waiting for the order.

They finally had to give up and return to England. There they had heard that the second plane had released its men according to plan. There had been clear moonlight where they had been released.

The third plane had not returned. They later heard that it had disappeared on the way over with all the boys who were to be released.

For a month Knut had been waiting for good weather. Time and time again he had taken to flight and each time something had gone wrong.

Finally he sailed down through the air and landed near Oslo. Here he had the unfortunate fate of being involved in the liquidation of the female informer.

It was probably here that the most important reason for Knut's breakdown had to be sought.

Freddy tried to tell the whole story as correctly as possible.

He himself felt being carried away by his emotions. It felt like he was talking about himself. He tried to get the doctor to sense all the horror and fear that Knut had had to go through. Always afraid of something. Afraid to fly, even more afraid to parachute. Afraid of being caught by the Gestapo, afraid that he wouldn't be able to keep up. Afraid of the terrible shame of not daring to go to work.

Most of all he was afraid of dying. Year after year that horror had followed him. He had somehow managed to control himself, keep himself under control. But his already worn-out nervous system could not handle the strain of liquidating the young woman.

He had always had to burn inside with the terrible secret. The two boys who were with him at work were later killed by the Germans. Knut had known that one had actually been picked apart, limb by limb as revenge for the bestial murder that the Gestapo had called the liquidation of the woman. Knut had known that the Germans knew that he had been involved in the job, and he was fully aware that if he was caught, he could thank his God for his mercy if he could die fairly quickly.

'This is the story, doctor,' said Freddy. 'If there is any person on this earth who really has reason to break down it is a fellow like Knut. And if he were to end up in prison he is most certainly hopelessly lost.'

The doctor had long ago stopped eating. He lit a cigarette, offered one to Fruen and the other two and then stood up:

'I will find out where he is now,' he said.

A while later he returned.

'I have spoken to the police doctor. There is no doubt that this has nothing to do with crime but Knut is very bad. I intend to drive down and see him right away.'

'They can join,' he said to Freddy, 'but there will be too many with four.'

Freddy asked if he should drive the doctor, but he had his own car.

Freddy gave Harald the key to the Opel and agreed to meet in the Club afterwards. Harald was supposed to drive Fruen back home, so Freddy and the doctor drove.

At *No. 19* they met the police doctor. Freddy greeted him and together they were followed into a cell. There Knut was lying on the bed. He seemed fairly calm now but was very pale. Freddy patted him on the shoulder and Knut began to cry. He cried more and more.

The police doctor and the doctor went out into the hallway and started talking.

Freddy stroked Knut's hair:

'So Knut, take it easy now. Try to tighten up a bit. Nothing has happened and it's only trifles compared to all that crap during the war.' It was as if Knut was listening to Freddy. He finally got control of himself and lay still.

'Are you able to talk to the doctor now,' Freddy asked. 'I've explained everything to him and you have to remember that it's not just you who have bloody memories of the rat catching. I struggle with the same thing you know that, but we have to get through it. Just lay your cards on the table. Tell everything. There is talk of you getting a longer sea voyage as recreation. My God Knut, you've cracked but it's only temporary.'

'But what is it that I have done,' asked Knut.

Freddy didn't get to answer because just then the doctor came in.

Knut asked if he could stay laying down. The doctor looked at him a little, felt for his pulse, and then sat down on the bed.

'Freddy has told me quite a lot about you. I need to know everything that is pressing if I am to be able to help,' he said. 'I know that you have been one of those who had the job of liquidating during the war and I understand that people like you, who have been involved in such things, find it difficult to forget the old memories. Isn't that right?'

'Yes, almost,' whispered Knut, 'but it's not just that. I haven't been able to sleep for a long time and not being able to sleep is horrible. And when I finally fall asleep I always dream the same thing over and over again.'

'What are you dreaming about?' asked the doctor.

It's difficult to explain,' said Knut. 'It's like I'm standing on a big patch of mud. I stand on a rock in the middle of the sea of mud. All around me, mud is steaming. It stinks, and it's as if this whole sea of mud consists of nothing but excrement. The lighting is reddish and brown. All around me, heads keep sinking so that only their hair floats up. And there are always women's heads. It's so disgusting with the big hair that sinks into the mud. Then there is a woman's head in front of me. It's bloody and bruised and its eyes wide and wild with terror.'

Here Knut stopped, and they had to wait until he regained control of his emotions, he continued:

'Then a long skinny arm comes out of the mud and tries to grab my leg. I stand there and try and kick her in the face. I try to push her into the mud. I put my foot on her head and push her down. The mud fills her mouth and eventually her head slides under, but the big hair floats on top of the mud. The skinny arm grabs my leg and pulls me into the mud and down in a perpetual spiral as I suffocate. I try and fight back but I sink and sink.'

'Finally I can't move, then the woman's face appears from the mud. Now she is no longer afraid but evil and hideous to look at. She opens her mouth and I see that she has sharp flat teeth like the cannibals have. Mud flows out of her mouth. Her eyes are empty and white worms come out of them. She rises from the mud and it turns out that it's her arms that have a hold of me. She pushes me further down. I feel the terrible taste of mud and I'm choking. Then I always wake up freezing cold and drenched in sweat. I often scream and wake people up.'

Knut lay with his face against the wall and spoke monotonously and in a low voice.

'Do you think much about the liquidation on the bridge Knut?' asked the doctor.

'Yes,' said Knut, 'every moment, day and night.'

'I will never forget it. God forbid I'd never been a part of it! God grant that I had never been in the fight against the Germans.'

'I am not fit for such a thing. I'm always much too scared. I get sick from seeing blood.'

'As a child, I made a long lance from an umbrella arrow which I put on a long stick and then I was going to kill a cat. I crawled under the barn until I had the cat cornered under the barn floor. I lay there and stabbed it. The cat howled as I stabbed and I cried. Finally I ran home and went to bed to cry. The cat was lying under the floor and howling when I later rescued it.'

'I was completely distraught but managed to drag it out. Then I saw the damage I had done. It was wounded everywhere. And then, when I would have given anything to save it, the farm boy had to beat it to death with an axe and then I got a beating.'

'Some of the same feelings I had at a liquidation. I felt it was wrong to kill the girl on the bridge. I panicked. It was the same again. Just like the time with the cat, when I went from being a bold hunter to panicking and crying with pity, and then regretting it terribly afterwards.'

'This is how it was with the girl on the bridge. I regretted so terribly that we had taken her.'

'At first we had planned the whole thing carefully and it was fine. None of us had ever been involved in killing a human being. I had once seen a mate get killed because his parachute didn't deploy. That was all the knowledge I had of death. For two days we had this woman with us, and for two days I was panicking about what was going to happen.'

'I'm sure the other two felt the same way. I just kept wishing for her to get a chance to escape or for the *Gestapo* to come. But nothing happened and in the end we drove out to the bridge.'

'What happened out there before I can't forget. And last night it just clicked for me as I understand. I don't really remember what happened last night.'

'Were you very fond of the girl you visited last night?' asked the doctor.

Knut did not answer immediately.

Then he said:

'Perhaps I was happier in the security I felt when I was with her. I can say that I was fond of her. I am often afraid of being alone. What happened last night, I don't know.'

The doctor said that he would like to be alone with Knut for a bit and Freddy went outside. He paced back and forth in the hall and smoked a cigarette.

He thought of the boys in Scotland for whom it had flipped. He remembered once he had seen that they had come with a large Norwegian who was completely rebellious. He had shouted and screamed and it had caused a sick feeling when they carried him from the ambulance onto the train to London.

Knut seemed completely normal now, but last night he had been dangerous. They probably had to keep him locked up. But they could perhaps get him into a better clinic where he could be more comfortable.

Thank God that there were no such conditions here as he had seen in Cuba. What had happened at that time was completely incomprehensible to Freddy. He had probably been drunk and violent and had been in a fight. But from there to being put in a madhouse was a long leap. Although when you consider that in this country the insane are put in prison or put in the drunken detention centre, it is no surprise.

It was awful to think about what he had experienced in that cage where a whole bunch of insane people had wandered around screaming. If he had found himself in that situation today, where his nervous system was completely worn out, he would certainly have gone completely crazy within a short time.

It was therefore about saving Knut from being locked up in an ordinary asylum. If only it were possible to get him out on such a sea voyage as Fruen spoke of?

The doctor came to the door:

'You get to say goodbye to your mate. For the time being I will arrange for him to be sent to hospital for observation.'

Freddy asked Knut if he wanted anything:

'Yes please. Do you have any smoke?'

The doctor was in a hurry and Freddy went over to the Club where he met Harald. He told them what had happened and said that now all they had to do was settle down and wait for the doctor to examine him properly. They managed to send him some reading material and a smoke.

Freddy came to think that now there was no other way out. He had to see to it that he got home and got everything sorted out with Miriam. He dreaded it terribly but it had to be done.

CHAPTER 13

At the gate he met Mrs. Olsen. She smiled slyly and said that there were some who were lucky and could finish work so early in the day because he came from work now, didn't he?

Freddy answered: 'Yes,' and went up the stairs. He unlocked the door and went inside.

Miriam was sitting in bed. She had a bed full of magazines such as *Romanjournalen* and *Alle Kvinner.* She also had a glass with something in it that seemed to have come from a port wine bottle that was on the table.

She didn't greet Freddy but just continued reading. She took a sip:

'Toast! Miriam,' she said.

Freddy saw that she had probably had a lot to drink.

Suddenly she said to Freddy:

'Yes! You dare to venture home at this time. You must have worn yourself out with business as usual I imagine,' she continued ironically. 'But by all means don't stop, you, my boy. Don't pay any attention to me I'm doing just fine!'

I should just say it, Freddy thought, but it was damn hard to get started.

'Knut went crazy last night,' he said suddenly. 'He is now confined at *No. 19* but will presumably be admitted to hospital for observation.'

He could have bitten off his tongue when he said that. It had nothing to do with the case and nothing to do with Miriam.

'Which Knut?' Miriam asked.

'You remember Knut, whom you met in the Club at the cocktail party that was held when Yngvar travelled to Australia.'

'Oh, yes, the dark one who got really drunk right?

Freddy couldn't remember him getting that drunk but agreed with Miriam that it was probably him. Miriam was interested now and Freddy had to tell her that Knut had come home and found that there was another man with his girl etc.

Freddy was furious with himself for being so foolish and talking about Knut instead of getting straight to the point. But Miriam was fiercely interested now so Freddy stood there talking and talking instead of getting to what he had come home for.

'Aren't you tired my dear?' said Miriam. Are you coming to bed?'

She made inviting room for him in bed and Freddy noticed to his great dismay that even now, when he was so full of Gerd, Miriam still had a certain erotic attraction to him as she lay in bed tempting him with her perky breasts and voluptuous form.

Freddy decided to get straight to the point:

'I think that we should split up and go our separate ways,' he said.

'What do you mean?'

'I think we should separate. We don't fit together Miriam. You know that, and in the long run it's silly of you to waste your time with me.' Miriam pulled the nightgown a little further up around her, she actually had to press one breast under the dress to get it in place. Then she took a sip from the glass.

'I'm surprised to hear that from you Freddy. I've often thought about it myself when I've been lying here at home waiting for you through the night. Now you think that we can just part ways and say thank you for a pleasant time together, or sex if you like. Because it's probably only what has interested you.'

Freddy didn't answer.

'It's not certain that it will be that easy. Imagine if we had children, or what would you do if I were to have a child? '

Miriam suddenly pulled the covers up over her and hid her head, and Freddy heard her crying. Freddy felt himself completely stiff from the shock. He saw all his plans with South America and Gerd fall to pieces. Miriam was going to have a child. It was clear that it was going to happen. I guess it was the course of nature that she wasn't going to let him go so easily. Freddy knew that whatever he did, he must not sit down on her bed. If he now gave in to his sympathy for her it wouldn't be long before he slept with her again.

'Miriam,' he said harshly. 'Let's talk about this. I am determined that we will divorce. It's no use continuing. Our marriage has been a big misunderstanding. You are right that it is mainly my fault. I've basically never felt anything for you other than erotic attraction. And that is too weak a foundation for a marriage.'

He swallowed deeply and asked her:

'Are you pregnant Miriam?'

She didn't answer but he heard that she had stopped crying.

He lit a cigarette.

'Miriam. Let's look at this sensibly. I'm leaving you whether I get a divorce or not.'

Miriam got up in bed and took her bag which was on the table next to her. She fished out a powder and a mirror and powdered herself a little.

'You're a pig Freddy, and in a way I'm glad to get rid of you. You think you can just do whatever you want. It would be really nice if you could just marry a girl, but you don't, you use her as a place for your semen, and then when you want a nice new place, you walk away from her.'

'Oh no. You talked about Knut being crazy. Do you think you are somewhat more normal? Don't you think I've seen you at night when you have your contractions? Do you think you seem the least bit normal when you stand up in bed against the wall talking about rat catching and how you're going to kill the next person? Don't you think I know you killed an old man with an umbrella? How many times do you think you've been talking in your sleep about how you were just shooting and he wouldn't fall but just stood there waving his umbrella? Don't you think I understood that you were the kind of wild pig who during the war took any opportunity to kill? Any idiot must understand that you wouldn't run around with a gun if it wasn't because you're afraid you'll suffer from it one day. You talk about Knut going crazy, you're not a hair better are you? To me you can do whatever you want as long as you pay. But you can bet it won't be cheap. Don't think I'm going to be the object of ridicule and shame in front of everyone with your baby and then perhaps have to toil and drag to get money for food.'

Freddy looked at Miriam and only now did he understand that she was not only foolish and conceited but also malicious.

'When you put it that way Miriam there's no point in discussing the matter at all. Think about it. I'm not kidding. If you don't agree to a divorce, I'll just go my way.

And that whatever you're going to have…'

Freddy stopped himself. It was difficult for him to say 'a child or not.'

He left. When he got a little way down the stairs he heard Miriam call out to him:

'Freddy, come back up! Oh Freddy, don't go!'

Freddy stopped then turned and went back upstairs. He was surprised that Miriam was not crying.

'I'm sorry for everything I said Freddy, especially about your dreams. Of course I'm proud of your efforts. But I'm so unhappy these days and I can't bear the thought of losing you. Can't we try again? If we only had an apartment, I'm sure everything would be fine again because there's no one else you've fallen in love with is there Freddy?'

Freddy felt that it would be impossible to tell her about Gerd. He told her he didn't think it would help if they got a new apartment. They were not compatible and he was determined to get a divorce. Miriam finally tried to be reasonable and Freddy insisted that they were to get a divorce. It had all been a big misunderstanding. He also told her that she must be able to arrange it so that she did not have children. He felt that he was being brutal when he said that but now that he had started there was no going back. He had to carry it out. He had to become a free man. Miriam looked at him but said nothing.

'I will try to manage it financially so you don't suffer

any hardship but you have to start working again. Damn it too, Miriam. You talk to me as if I've ruined your life and I get the feeling that I'm the one who talked you into this idiotic marriage of ours, but you know in your heart that it's also your fault that we got married. You haven't lost anything by it. You can go straight back to your job.'

'The situation is different now Freddy,' Miriam interrupted him.

Freddy felt his anger rise within him. Heck, but he controlled himself:

'Get dressed, then we'll have lunch out somewhere, we can then discuss the whole thing when we calm down.'

Miriam stood up and poured water into a wash basin then took off her nightgown. Freddy looked at her disinterestedly. He actually felt disgusted looking at her body. She washed under her arms with a cloth and he thought to himself that the best proof that they weren't a match was that he didn't like her smell.

He suddenly thought of an experience he had had in England once during the war. He had been on leave in Dublin. It would have been wonderful after three months of hard training to be able to check into a first-class hotel and know that he had several days ahead of him where all he had to do was sleep, eat, drink and go to the cinema, enjoying himself according to all the rules of art. He had plenty of money. It had been a great hotel and there was good music for tea dances in the afternoon.

Freddy had been friendly to the whole world and had seen a lovely lady sitting alone at a table, he had been asked by the waiter if he could have a dance with her. It was war, he was in uniform and the lady said yes with a small nod. They had danced and later had a drink together. They had dinner together and he called himself a lucky pig who had gotten hold of such a pretty girl on the first day. He had got very excited about her and when he followed her up to her room in the evening he had been allowed to go in with her and he ended up staying in bed with her.

So far nothing had happened other than what any soldier dreamed would happen when he got his leave. Suddenly someone unlocked the door, the light switched on and two men were standing there looking at Freddy and the lady he was in bed with.

Freddy was furious and asked if they hadn't realised that they had entered the wrong room.

Suddenly the woman got up in bed - without a thread on her body, and started screaming. Freddy tried to drag her back into bed but was badly affected by the whole situation. His clothes were scattered all over the room. One of the guys came over to the bed and red in his face screamed at Freddy to pack up and get out of his hotel.

The other guy was a tall fellow in a naval officer's uniform, and suddenly it had dawned on Freddy that he was lying there in bed with a naval officer's wife. The situation was insane, after all it's not easy to start a fight without any clothes on. And Freddy couldn't for the life of him find his trousers.

The woman sat up and screamed. She got out of bed and went straight towards the window. Freddy grabbed her hair and pulled her back into bed. During all the screaming and the spectacle the tall naval officer had just stood there and watched.

The little fat The little fat man he'd given a slap had started tugging at Freddy's arm. man he'd given a slap had started tugging at Freddy's arm. He had finally found his trousers and put them on. The worst part was that in the confusion his English had become even worse. But at least he was now able to tell the hotel manager that he could the hell get out of there. That this was a matter that did not concern him. Freddy's heart began to beat faster as he thought about trying to explain to the naval officer that he had no idea that the woman had been married.

The man had helped him to find his clothes and then had opened the door for him and said:

'I understand. You have nothing to do with this, I don't blame you for it either. Good night!'

Freddy looked back at the terrified woman in bed. He wondered what to do, but he had left, like a dog with its tail between its legs. The next day when he asked for the bill he had the feeling that everyone was laughing at him.

No, Freddy had a certain ability to get lost in stories

with women but this time it was considerably worse.

Miriam was now ready and they headed out down the street. They didn't talk much until they were sitting in a restaurant and had ordered the food. Miriam said:

'How are your finances? Would you rather settle for divorce now, or what? Tell me Freddy, do you have anyone else in your sights? You don't plan on remarrying do you?'

'No,' Freddy lied, 'I think it would probably be best if we divorced, if I can manage it, but if you're pregnant the whole thing will be desperately different. Would you keep the child Miriam?'

He realised at once that it was a foolish question and Miriam did not want to answer the question either. Instead she asked him what he intended to do. Whether he wanted to go to the gold mines in Colombia or had other plans.

Freddy spoke a great deal about the gold mines in Colombia and that he intended to work over there for a few years to get some money. Here at home there was no chance for a young man who wanted to get ahead in life.

They were now sitting and talking quietly together. Miriam loved going to restaurants and she kept a close eye on everything that was going on. She always had to try and catch the eyes of the men who came within range and it was very uncomfortable for Freddy, but now he told himself it doesn't matter. In a short time she would probably go out to some restaurant with a friend, and then she would sit and try and catch the eye of some handsome man. There would certainly be contact and sooner or later she would have a permanent following.

Freddy sat and tried to construct an image that he knew deep down wasn't entirely true. It was very possible that Miriam could make a good wife for the right man but he was not the right one, and their start had been as bad as it could possibly be. Miriam did not fit into the difficult conditions of fighting for everything. In order to get an apartment and the struggle to get Freddy to stop drinking, she had not been a good fit. She had been like a bitch on heat, desperate to make use of the time with him.

He often thought of a female writer who had been mentioned by a critic as an erotic steamroller. Miriam was big and delicious. Her body certainly required exercise, but when, instead of work and exercise, she just lay in bed around the clock, she burned inside with an immeasurable energy that she could only release during sexual intercourse.

'What a stylish *New Look*,' said Miriam suddenly and pointed with a nod towards a lady who entered the restaurant.

Freddy saw that it was the *Lady*, and really hoped that she would not see them, or worse, that Miriam would recognise her. They had been with her once at a party and Miriam had kept insisting that they should try to get together with the stylish people again.

They remained undetected, Miriam was supposedly

188

only concerned with the wife's *New Look*. Soon after this Freddy paid the bill and they left the restaurant. Miriam had a couple of errands she wanted to run and Freddy therefore wanted to go home to take a nap. He felt tired deep in his soul.

CHAPTER 14

Gerd stopped typing on the typewriter for a moment. She grabbed her purse and took out a cigarette.

As usual she had worked hard all morning. Through the endless rows of short-hands, the monotonous ticking of the typewriter, the whining of the traitor being interrogated and all the boring routine work, she had only had one thought in her head, namely Freddy.

She was completely sick with longing for him and scared to death that he would change his mind. She had imagined in her mind how Miriam had persuaded Freddy again, and she had hated the thought of what could happen at Freddy's house now. She had gone through all the agonies imaginable, from jealousy to self-pity, fear of having children and being let down by Freddy. Now she sat fantasising about giving birth to a lonely and abandoned child, and she saw in her mind how she would create a small, pleasant home for herself and the child.

Gerd tore herself out of her daydreams and laughed to herself. Then she laughed even more. She felt that she was about to start crying.

She turned and saw a man sitting and looking at her with wide eyes. My God, she had completely forgotten that she had a defector waiting for her.

She picked up her handkerchief and wiped her eyes.

'Excuse me,' she said, 'would you like a cigarette?'

She offered him one from her packet.

He mumbled something about it being kind way too much and then he took a cigarette with a lustful expression in his eyes. She lit the cigarette for him. He quickly took a couple of puffs and then he sucked in a long, long puff.

She saw him change and become completely relaxed. He lit up and said:

'They have no idea miss, what it means to be completely crazy with nicotine hunger and then to sit and watch others smoke. Thank you for the cigarette.'

Gerd looked at him. She felt like talking to him:

'You are married and have three children, right?'

'Yes, he said, I have the world's most beautiful three little girls.

Would you like to see a picture of them?'

He pulled out a letter and showed her two pictures. One with three wonderful little white haired girls. They were like three little dolls. They held each other's hands as if they were fending off all the evil in the world. The largest was in the middle and you could see that she had unconsciously taken on her mother's responsibility for the two smallest. All three had probably been a little afraid of the photographer.

'How old are they?' Gerd asked.

'She is the oldest in the middle, she is 8 years old. The other two are twins. They are 6 years old. The second picture is of my wife.'

Gerd saw a pretty, small, fair woman holding one of the twins in her arms while the other two held her by her skirt. The little woman was completely crushed under the weight of the child in her arms. She had a lovely, kind smile. It was as if the picture radiated harmony. Yet the father and husband sat here now as a defector.

Gerd suddenly became furious. How could he do what he did when he had such wonderful children?

He took the photographs back and quietly put them in the envelope and tucked them under his jacket into a pocket.

'I don't want to make excuses, miss. You have to believe me, I don't understand how I could mess up like I did and I knew all along that it was wrong. I understood that it would affect my wife and children. I wasn't blind, I knew that even if the Germans won the war my family would still be branded by other Norwegians, except perhaps NS members.'

'Today it's impossible for me to explain it all. I was crazy. I've always been interested in politics - I probably never understood any of it. I always loved criticising our government. I thought everything they did was wrong. I always liked to talk about how bad everything was up here in this crazy country. One day in a gentlemen's party, when I was posting as usual about how idiotic this and that was, and the latest scandal about our useless government, there was a man who told me that he completely agreed with me and that I should do like him and join the *NS*.'

'I wasn't enthusiastic about *Quisling*, (the leader of the *NS*), but it turned out that one day I was sat in the Bjørneviks Theatre and watched a meeting. A lot of good things were said. All the things that I used to use as arguments against the government were used. There were some mob boys who tried to make a noise, they were firmly thrown out. It was just like a comradely atmosphere inside the room, and that atmosphere appealed to me. There were uniforms and lots of flags. All the speeches were intense and one got a vivid impression that there was a burning love of country and idealism behind them.'

'We sang patriotic songs and stood upright. I was taken over by the moment. I remember seeing people crying and I myself had a big lump in my throat. When the meeting was over we went out into the street where large crowds had gathered.'

'They whistled us out. Swear words were shouted. A youngster knocked my hat off and before I knew it I was in a full-on brawl. The police came and broke up the crowd. I had come together with some *NS* supporters and we almost felt like crusaders as we walked across the street after the battle. My new friends came home with me. My wife and I were newly-weds. We all sat up into the night talking politics, and we agreed that something had to be done to save Norway. The *NS* was the way.'

Gerd offered him another cigarette, she lit it and took one for herself.

'Carry on,' she said, 'we have plenty of time.'

'You understand, that after that day I was more eager than most. I went to all the meetings that there were. I soon ended up at the lectern myself and could then talk down on the ruling parties in front of a large audience.'

'You know my sad career.'

'The 9th April it fell apart for me. I signed up for service and I was amongst the first to open fire on the Germans. I tagged along and asked my captain for all the worst jobs. I had catching up to do.'

'Then hostilities ceased and I now heard that the English had failed us. Little by little all the poison from the propaganda seeped into me. I hated the government that had escaped to England with all the gold. Now they sat over there far from all the dangers, drinking whiskey and enjoying themselves. And it was they who were to blame for everything!'

'I saw how all the businessmen flew the Germans' errands to make money. Like everyone else, I was impressed by the German soldier. His discipline and how well behaved he was. I met my old comrades from the *NS*, and soon after I was at the meetings again. Not long after that I was stood on the podium again and lashed out at the government who was to blame for all the misery.'

'I should have listened to my wife. She cried the day I proudly came home and said I had given my speech. I was already completely crazy. I became absolutely furious when even war profiteers, who were not afraid to appear in a restaurant with a German, would not greet me.'

'I also started to name people. I wanted to force them to recognise me and the party. At the time I was so sure we were right.'

'During that time I was never with the Germans. They were our enemies. I was convinced that it was important for the Norwegian people to remain good friends with them at all costs and ensure that we in the *NS* were allowed to rule the country. There was no doubt in my mind that the war was already decided. The Germans had to win, and we in the *NS* wanted to save our country. We were the only ones who could create an independent Norway again.'

'Russia joined the war and I was inflamed by the crusader mentality and the desire to fight against the Bolsheviks. We remembered so well little Finland's desperate fight against the Russians. The time when all of Norway sympathised with the Finns, and we sent all the help we could manage. We also sent volunteers and I remembered when one winter's day I had stood down at the railway station and said goodbye to a friend of mine who was traveling as a volunteer. Norwegian military had turned up at the station.'

'There were speeches and patriotic songs. We sang The national anthem, *Ja vi elsker,* and afterwards I shook the hands of my comrades in arms from the *NS* and solemnly promised that I would join.'

'I never got that far. The atmosphere changed for the worse not long after I left.'

'This time it was true that the German military showed up, but patriotic songs were also sung and *Ja vi elsker* echoed through the station premises. We stood there with tears in our eyes wanting to get started and sacrifice our lives for our beloved fatherland.'

Gerd looked at the defector. He looked past her out the window with a small bitter smile on his face.

'I guess I experienced the same as other soldiers. It may have happened that my thoughts wandered and I thought that perhaps there is a Norwegian soldier on the other side willing to sacrifice his life for his beloved fatherland Norway.'

'I remember playing with the idea that one day the Norwegian soldier on the other side and I would meet in battle. We would drive our bayonets into each other and then we would look at each other's uniforms. One an English uniform, the other a German, but we both wanted a small Norwegian flag on the shoulder and it would say Norway above the flag.'

'We both wanted to idealistically fight for the same cause, namely Norway's freedom. And we would both die for the same cause. But in each other's eyes we would be traitors to the country.'

'I got through the hell up there alive and I learned to appreciate my comrades, their willingness to sacrifice, their efforts and good camaraderie. The more I got to know the Germans the more I hated them.'

'Later I was transferred south, to Norway again. It was awful to feel the hatred and contempt from the bastards. I could go wild with rage at times and it was especially after it began to dawn on me that I had been an idiot. And what was worse was that I had committed a crime against my country and helped the country's enemies. I would never even admit it to myself but I knew it all the time. Sometimes the thought crossed my mind that I should make contact with the other side - with the bastards.'

'I knew that I could be of great use. My little attempts were only met with contempt and suspicion from my old friends from before the war. Then I told myself it was a shame to leave the sinking ship and I continued as a member until the end.'

'I see from your papers that you are accused of having shot a Norwegian patriot during the war,' said Gerd. 'So it had nothing to do with the Bolsheviks? Or your patriotism?'

The traitor looked down. Then he ran his hand through his hair.

'No,' he said, 'that's where I sinned and you can imagine I'll be punished enough for that.'

'After I returned from the front I was given command of a patrol that was supposed to patrol the streets of Oslo. We examined people and cars to find traces of saboteurs and terrorists. We also helped the Germans and the state police with their raids.'

'It's horrible to think about, but for us it was just exciting and we always hoped that it would become *something,* as we said.'

'One day we experienced *something.* We were involved in a raid. Suddenly we heard several shots and saw a man come running out. We realised it was a saboteur, I opened fire and hit him and he fell to the ground. Another man came out of the door and we all now opened fire. We shot like crazy and continued even after he was sprawled out on the ground.'

Then another guy came towards us with a gun in his hand shooting at us. We all got down as the fellow got to a plank fence which he jumped over. As he disappeared over the fence I fired at him.'

'We found the guy behind the fence. He was a young

blonde fellow. My shot had hit him in the spine and had paralysed his lower body. He had dragged himself away a little and then opened fire when he saw us. One of our guys got hit and I had to tell them to be careful. I gave a message that they had to block off the street on the other side so he wouldn't escape.'

'The saboteur was a hard nut to crack. Every time we tried to get near him he fired. Finally I got an aim on him and fired. It went quiet. We didn't approach him but waited and waited.'

'Finally we heard a voice shouting: *God save the king and the fatherland,* and then he started singing the first words of *Ja vi elsker - Yes we love.* We were stood flabbergasted and waited for what he would come up with next.'

'Then we heard the voice turn into a moan. We heard him trying to move, then there was complete silence. We shouted for him to surrender but got no answer. Eventually I ventured all the way to where he lay and there I found the terrible saboteur, the criminal, whom we had so eagerly chased down. He was dead. I looked at him as he lay drenched in his own blood. My last shot had smashed his shoulder and disabled his right arm. He was as Norwegian as anyone could be. Completely fair with very curly hair.'

'When I turned him a little I saw that he was still alive. He had clear blue eyes staring at me, full of contempt. It was as if he wanted to say something, then he had a convulsion and immediately afterwards his heart stopped beating. I guessed that he had taken poison.'

'Some Germans arrived. A couple of police officers congratulated me on getting him. Then it dawned on me in all its horror what I had done. My little thought experiment from the front that I should drive the bayonet into a Norwegian patriot had worked. The boy who was now lying there in front of me with two of my bullets in him was Norwegian. He had fought for what I had imagined I was fighting for, namely Norway's freedom. Now we, his enemies, stood over him. We who imagined that we were idealists and fought for the only right thing, suddenly discovered that we were standing there, shoulder to shoulder with Norway's enemies, namely the Germans.'

'We enjoyed the triumph over the enemy who had died with *Ja vi elsker dette landet - Yes we love this country.* Afterwards we went over to look at the other saboteur that we had shot. He was completely peppered from all the bullets.'

'My comrades congratulated me on my championship shot, but I knew I had sinned. I now knew that the others were right. They fought for what was right. The rest of us fought for the Germans. We used the Nazi salute. We died for our great leader, while the others could die with Yes, we love on their lips - the lyric to the Norwegian Anthem.'

'Now began a terrible time for me. I regretted it so terribly. I told my wife all about it, and we agreed that when the war was over, we would try to track down the parents of the young boy and explain my guilt. If we could help them, we would.'

'Unfortunately, I was too weak to do anything positive towards the others during the rest of the war. It was like hell and few people were as happy as I was when liberation came. I was determined not to defend myself. I have no objections either. I totally accept that I am punished for the wrongs I have done, the years I have left of the punishment will pass. My wife is waiting for me. Once I am free, I will never meddle in politics again. I will try to make up for what I have done wrong.'

Gerd had sat quietly and listened to the traitor. She had also looked out of the window at the sky, which was now a clear blue autumn sky. She thought of that poor devil who had ended up taken his own life.

She thought she knew who it was. She was sure Freddy knew him.

'Does it bother you to think about that boy?' she asked.

It took a while before he answered, but then he uttered with a low voice:

'There is no point in explaining how I suffer from the memory of it. I always see his face with those blue eyes staring at me in contempt. I can't forget it. At night as I walk back and forth in the cell I see someone staring at me from the darkness. I talk to him and sometimes I think I'm going crazy. I'm basically very normal and I long like a wild person to get out into the wonderful world and rebuild my home. And you can be sure that I will never meddle in politics again for the rest of my life.'

'I understand more and more that politics is a curse that causes brothers to drive the knife into each other. And you can be convinced that many of our worst Nazis are actually fine people who would normally never hurt a cat.'

'They are fanatical idealists. Now and then I feel that idealists, at least the patriotic ones, are a curse to humanity. It takes so little before war breaks out.'

Gerd had a feeling that the man was at least telling the truth, but at the same time she was a little confused:

'There is one thing I don't quite understand, and that is how you could take part in the war against the Germans in 1940 and then afterwards help them oppress the rest of us? Did the abuses from the *NS* never disgust you? They must have left a bad taste in your mouth all the time? You must have known then that what you did was criminal?'

The traitor looked at her calmly. Then he said:

'They know that today we have a party in this country that is based on fanatical members who would take over the role we had during the war. They will help the country's enemies. But even among them, there are blinded idealists who believe that they are fighting for the only right. And many bright-eyed patriots will surely end up killing each other in the sure belief that they, individually, are doing the only right thing, and that they are fighting for Norway's freedom. It is no use for a normal person to try to understand what drives an insane person to commit a crime, and I was insane with idealism.'

'We will experience the same thing again. Young men will kill each other out of idealism and love of the same country.'

'I'm done with it forever. It's all false and hollow to me. I've been convicted as a traitor, a defector. I have failed my country for sure, but what's worse is that I've let down my three young children and my wife, and that's the worst for me.'

The phone rang. Gerd took it, and answered:

'I'll come right away.'

'Well it was very interesting to hear your story,' Gerd concluded. 'I believe you. I can only regret that you cannot benefit from the amnesty. You have received a longer sentence than the time included under the amnesty. However, I think you have to admit that you deserve that punishment from our point of view?'

The defector said nothing, but thanked her for the cigarette. Gerd called out to the constable in the next room who immediately came in and took over.

Gerd quickly finished writing some papers and then went in to see the representative who had called her. She had a lot to do for the rest of the day and was happy when she finally finished her work. She hurried home. She was hoping that Freddy would be outside, or that there was a message for her at home.

She found neither him nor a message. She greeted her hostess and chatted a little with her. They discussed the latest news and the chances of war, but agreed that there would be no war. Not yet, anyway.

Gerd lit a cigarette and laid down on the divan. She had to smile at her banter with the hostess. How idiotic it is to stand completely normal, restrained and calm and discuss whether there will be war or not. She felt that one should do something. No one in the whole world wants war. War today is just horrible. There is nothing romantic about it.

If we women seriously stepped in to abolish the war, it would perhaps help. As it is now, with hero worship and medals, idealism and confused patriotism, we would surely experience the same thing again. If only we women would use the weapons we have, thought Gerd.

Then she had to smile at the thought of the weapons.

For example, we could refuse to sleep with a military man.

She saw in her spirit all women and the whole world using the weapon against the military, and naturally then against the politicians. Although the politicians would perhaps not be hit so hard. They are probably too busy with their own ambitions.

A woman could be weak and it might not be so easy to use the weapon when it came to the man she loved. She thought of Freddy, and knew with herself that she wanted to be the obedient wife. She would love him whatever his political views. In a flash she understood the wives of the Nazis, who followed their men through thick and thin. No, it probably wasn't that easy.

Now she wanted to sleep a little. She felt deathly tired. She wanted to dream about Freddy. She tried to smell him on the couch. She removed the blanket and the top sheet. She sniffed between the sheets where he had been lying. Here he had loved her. Here they had merged into one. She could imagine his wonderfully warm body between her legs and arms. How wonderful it was to be loved by Freddy. She wanted to be kind to him and she was looking forward to bearing him a child.

She saw herself on the farm in Chile with a whole bunch of light-haired kids, standing on the steps of the house with a lovely garden, bursting with oranges and with palm trees behind her. Then she would wave to Freddy, her husband, who rode out to inspect the farm.

They wanted to forget Victoria Terrace, hapless

country traitors and *rat catching* - envy, war and all evil.

Just Freddy and her.

Gerd dreamed herself further and further away until she fell asleep.

CHAPTER 15

Miriam greeted Mrs. Olsen at the corner of Vibes gate and Bogstadveien. As usual, Mrs. Olsen was a little ironic and said that she had heard that Freddy was home from work today.

Miriam just greeted her and moved on. It amazed her how she stuck her nose into everything. And now this nonsense with Freddy. After all, she knew with herself that Freddy was right. They didn't fit together. Freddy was so different from everyone else she had been with. There was no fun with him anymore. He walked about always looking like a mournful funeral procession.

When she met Freddy he had been wild and crazy and always out to meet other people to try and get some fun out of life. They had gone from one party to the next. She had met a lot of nice people. For a time they had gone in and out of the finest houses in Oslo. She had been given a trip to Stockholm with Freddy, and it had been a great experience after the five long years of occupation to stay in a wonderful hotel and eat the world's most wonderful food. They had danced and gone to the opera and the theatre. They had had a wonderful time in Stockholm, and she had been very much in love with Freddy at the time.

Then the grey everyday life had started to creep in.

First there was the great disappointment of not getting a proper apartment and then Freddy had started to be very strange with her. It was just like he didn't like taking her with him to parties. She had once asked him directly if she wasn't good enough. If he was ashamed of her or what it was. In that case, it was his fault, because he didn't give her the opportunity to buy nice enough clothes.

Freddy had not answered, and she had also thought that it was silly to talk about clothes, because every time there was some gathering where the Lady or someone else invited them, it was always expressly pointed out that they should come in ordinary clothes.

Miriam knew there was something about her that Freddy disliked, but her intelligence did not stretch far enough to understand what it was. When Miriam was going to a party where there were people from the so-called better circles in Oslo, she did not understand that those people appreciated Freddy because he was an ordinary young man with a natural way of being and behaving. There were some influential people in Oslo who had an idea of what Freddy and his comrades had done during the war. As they themselves had taken their turn when it mattered, they would now like to see the guys well off, also financially.

It wasn't easy for Miriam when she came to a general gathering with her head full of ideas about how an educated lady of society should behave.

She always had her head full of stories from romantic magazines, where dramatic writers depicted receptions at court and with noble families in England. Firstly, there was a slight difference between what was written by such magazine writers and the reality, and secondly, there is a big difference between a larger reception at the society in England, and an ordinary, pleasant gathering with some nice people in Oslo. It is true that they have an old culture and are well off financially, but they have primarily learned to be ordinary and natural.

In such situations, Miriam played her role *on the stage* wonderfully. She refrained from showing reverence and saying *Your Highness,* but otherwise she kept the style she had read about. She was so beautiful and so formal that it was unbearable that she conversed and preened herself in all possible and impossible ways. If she had ever seemed simple, it was when she became snobbish and was trying to be part of. Freddy knew that it was impossible to explain anything to her, and he therefore chose not to take her with him when he visited the people he valued the most. No one ever asked for her and sometimes Freddy probably had a bad conscience.

As a rule, Miriam had always found some old sea dog who thought that Miriam's bulging bust and voluptuous forms were exciting. So Miriam, with her rich imagination in that area, had always imagined that when she returned home from such a successful evening, that she had been the queen of the night and the centre of attention. She had managed to cause a stir, more than Freddy cared about.

That existence was now over, and lately she had spent most of her time at home in the unattractive room. Freddy wanted to leave her. Yes, he could basically do that. It was just silly for her to waste her time on him.

Well, next time she would only marry someone who had a lot of money and who was willing to carry her through life. She mentally saw herself giving orders to the staff of servants lined up outside her palatial house as she got into her long black luxury carriage, held open by a smart chauffeur in uniform.

Miriam was so enlivened by the thought of this that she was in a very good mood when she let herself into the small, smelly corridor. Freddy was still asleep but jumped out of bed when the door opened. She could see that he had a violent heartbeat.

'Did I scare you my treasure?' he asked condescendingly.

Freddy laid back down and breathed heavily. He must have had a good nap but his heart was pounding. It was probably due to the state of his nerves.

He looked at his wristwatch.

'Geez, it's so late.'

Miriam hung up her hat and coat.

'It's a terrible chore to go shopping these days. You have to stand in a queue for hours, and then they have almost nothing when you finally get to the till.'

Freddy fetched a pitcher of water and had a wash. It freshened him up. He had little desire to start discussing with Miriam again. But she got into the question herself by saying that she wondered if he could get her a place to live, then she would be happy to move from Vidar's street. She didn't want to live here alone.

Freddy said he would try. Miriam sounded remarkably calm and composed. Perhaps she had now agreed with him that it was just as well to split up.

Damn it, too, that she might be pregnant!

'I'm going to see a friend of mine tonight so don't wait for me,' he said.

He felt in a good mood as he stood in the street. It had all worked out it seemed. He hurried over to a telephone booth and called Gerd. It was the hostess who answered the phone and when he asked for Gerd she said *one moment.*

Soon after he was speaking with Gerd. It was wonderful to hear her voice and he said a lot of stupid things into the phone.

Who would have thought that the tough *rat catcher* Freddy could say so much nonsense, but Gerd thought it was the most wonderful thing. They agreed to meet at a small restaurant.

Freddy ordered a drink while he waited for her. He did not have to wait long before she came. He wished he could have hugged and kissed her when she arrived but there were people around them and you did not do that now in a restaurant in Oslo.

Gerd asked for a glass of sherry. Afterwards they ordered dinner as she was hungry. They had half a bottle of wine with their meal and when a dark exotic looking lady came sailing up to the piano and began to play softly and pleasantly, they felt as if they were in seventh heaven.

Freddy enjoyed the intimate atmosphere, the music and having Gerd by his side and constantly being able to touch her. He enjoyed the conversation with her. It was so wonderful to be on the same wavelength. They had the same interests and they knew a lot of people together from the days of the war. Although they had said: *now we won't talk about the underground,* they soon switched to the things that had occupied them both for almost eight years.

Gerd told Freddy about the defector in the office and asked if he knew the two who had been shot.

Yes! Freddy knew the story and remembered well the boys he had been with in England. They had been here at home as instructors for *Milorg.*

Gerd told Freddy what the defector had said about blinded idealism and patriotism.

Freddy nodded.

'In many ways I agree,' he replied.

'And it's clear Gerd, that many, perhaps the majority of *NS,* were people who were ordinary good Norwegian citizens before they were carried away by these sick ideas.'

'The name *Nasjonal Samling,* was once wonderful,' said Freddy. 'Imagine if today we could had one party that called itself the *National Assembly* and they really wanted to bring everyone together to end the hatred between Norwegians. A party that could step in to get Norway back on its feet.'

'Wouldn't you be carried away by the idea of such a policy, a *National Assembly*? But the same thing would surely happen again. The leaders would run their own political game with their overriding desire for power and more power. And all of us little idealistic sheep would have to pay for their fun.'

'No Gerd, in the future we should only think about ourselves and not get involved in politics and idealism.'

Gerd laughed.

'Cheers Freddy, you can say all you want, but next time I think you'll be one of the first again. It's weird like that. Blood's thicker than water and you're very tied to Norway.'

'No, damn it,' said Freddy. 'We are traveling to South America, and the home we create there will become our fatherland. And I will gladly fight for that fatherland.'

'But not for all this shit here in Norway. After all, there has been nothing but jealousy and trouble since liberation. Every single day when you open the paper, there is someone new to be publicly slaughtered. Everyone looks down on everyone else.'

'The Norwegians who were in England looked down on those who were at home, and those who were at home, on those who were away, etc.'

'But now I'm starting all over again. However, one thing is certain Gerd, there is no country in the world apart from ours, which has shown such ingratitude towards its soldiers, and towards those who created Norway's name and goodwill. No nation has shown so little gratitude.'

'First they enticed the youth to make an *effort* as it was called. And when the war ended it was like a big merry-go-round that then stopped going around for the young people. They staggered about, completely dazed and dizzy, not knowing where they were, or where they wanted to go. But then the adults were there thank God, and they grabbed them and helped them back on to their feet, and thus everything was very wonderful.'

'But that was not the case with the Norwegian youth who came out of the carousel of the great war. They also stood there dazed and dizzy, not knowing where they wanted to go. They expected the adults to be there to help them. But no one gave them a helping hand. All the pleasure of the drive, mixed with horror and joy, was gone. Almost unconscious, they tried to find a way to get away, far away from the carousel. But everything just went round and round at tremendous speed, and wherever they turned there were new merry-go-rounds spinning around, but there weren't any adults there to hold their hands.'

Freddy smiled sadly:

'Now we are back in the same place again, Gerd. The only way I can manage to tear myself away from the memories of the war and everything related to it is to tell you something or other about my sinful youth before I met you. It will concentrate my mind.'

*****

APPENDIX I

Two books of Max' war memories appeared in Norway immediately after the war and became a huge sale's success. A few years later even an English edition existed. To give the reader a feeling of the atmosphere which ruled at the very first day after the liberation, I shall attach the following excerpt from his book **Underwater Saboteur:**

The Tables Turned

There was great excitement at Fritjof's when we trooped in in full uniform. Here there were more embraces. Brita Bigum, Bjørg Riiser Larsen, Else Heiberg and not least the maid Oline – all had taken their turn in the hard days when the Germans ruled over Norway. Now the town was aflame with fires of black-out curtains, and the people enjoyed seeing the light everywhere. It was peace.

But we could hear a banging a cracking down in the town. This was not all together unexpected. So now the fun was to begin. We jumped into the cars. We had two new cars now, while our ford was still in Fritjof's garage. But there was no reason for getting mixed up in things that were going on just in order to take part in something. To that extent the whole business was serious. At all costs we must not irritate the Germans. Once we did have trouble with the Germans – or, to be more correct, one of us did, and the result was one German dead and one wounded and a good chance of more fuss than was necessary. I therefore withdrew my troops to the aquavit bottles at Fritjof's, where they would celebrate the first meeting with peace. I myself drove down to Møllergata 19, where I met Captain Blindheim, a comrade of ours from the U.K. who was operational chief of D13 (Oslo). He was right in the thick of things and had been carrying on for God know how long. He looked tired. Orderlies were coming and going all the time, and the telephone rang unceasingly.

It was pleasant to see Svein Blindheim sitting there and directing the course of affairs. I had been his second in command in Scotland for a long and difficult period, but that was long ago. It was a good thing now that he was a capable military man who could exercise command. Svein was as friendly as usual and promised to make arrangements for me to meet 24 and the rest of the Oslo gang. I got hold of a few helmets and drove home to Fritjof's villa at Vinderen. But first I went for a turn up in the Slottspark to see a little of what was go- ing on there. There were shots at regular intervals. The Home Front boys told me that there had been some trouble, and that there were a lot of drunken Germans running about and brandishing their weapons.

While we were talking, two youngish German soldiers came down Karl Johan from the Drammen road. They had their uniforms open at the neck, and were drunk. They were both carrying revolvers, and it was quite an amusing moment when they passed me. They went past and down into the park, where they knew that they would be arrested by their own police. The situation in Oslo was fantastic. There were only German sol-diers and Norwegian Home Front boys. We had no authority to disarm the Germans but we could do what we liked with our own Nazis, and the Home Front looked after them.

It was late in the night now, and I drove home to Fritjof's to get some hour's sleep. But it was hard to sleep. The impression of the day raced through my brain. All the evening, when I was out driving, I had been stopped by Home Front soldiers on guard duty. Their discipline was incredibly good. Thousands, I am sure, lay sleepless that night as I did. My thoughts circled all the time round one point: "Now the worst was over; now at any rate we can fight openly; it is now we who will carry pistols for all to see." It was very pleasant to think that now the State police and Gestapo would have to go into hiding and use false papers. Now at last the time had come for an exchange of roles in everything. We represented law and order.

But the Gods alone know how things would have gone with us in those first days if the Germans had decided to fight. We and our Sten guns were just a drop in the ocean, and the Sten gun is a very bad weapon in war. But we had 8,000 police troops in Sweden, ready to move in. They were certainly on their way already. These lads knew their job; they were soldiers. When all the men from Sweden came, it would be of great help. They were equipped with the best weapons that could be produced, and they were thoroughly trained. They were all idealists who had had to flee the country when it grew too hot for them - just like ourselves. It was an impossibility to be in Milorg from the start and still live at home legally, if one had been in the least active.

On May 9 I was in the thick of it with the Oslo gang. No. 24 appeared with tree stars on his collar, and I clicked my heels together and saluted rigidly. He was the chief. Now a wonderful time began. We established our head quarters in the minister Blehr's villa, which we decided was classy enough for us. So it was here that the operation branch of the central organisation had its headquarters. Rolf had his own gang of fifty men in Pensionat Norum, which was only a few minutes' walk from us.

Arrests took place all around the clock. I was involved in one false alarm after the other. People rang us up and told us that a party of though front-fighters had dug themselves in somewhere. Someone bellowed "turn out!," and we left our whiskies, jumped straight into our cars, and raced through the town with our horns blowing all the time. Ambulances, fire engines and police cars could just pack up! The driving in Oslo in those days was absolutely mad. Oslo was mad. People just stood and shouted hurrah- at any rate those who had any voice left. Those who had lost their voices actually painted the word "hurrah" on placards. Down at Møllergata 19, the prison, there were always crowds of people cheering when Nazies were brought in.

Of course we had some queer experiences. We heard that the Gestapo had arranged false navy passports, and that ships in the port were full of Gestapo. We sat off at night with 300 Milorg boys to carry out a raid on all the ships. The chief of the criminal police, L'Abbée-Lund, came with us, and the police were accompanied by a little crowd of informers and Gestapo. It was quite incredible, but it was true. The Germans were eager to denounce one another, and we made good use of them. Some of the German Gestapo men came with us wearing masks.

The notorious Nazi 1, who had been on our list so long, and whom we had unsuccessfully tried to kill several times, was there to. Egil Halle went up to him and reminded him that he had kicked Vesla (his wife). The tables were turned now. I had a long look at him. He looked away, and I could see that he was trembling. Nazi 1, one of the big men, one of those whom we would have shot out of hand if we had come across him! He was smarter than most of the others. He was famous for his power of remembering faces, and this power he now placed at our disposal. He was ready to denounce his wife, his children, his mother. He would sell his best friend if it would help him to get an extra cigarette. Now he cringed and wagged his tail. But there was something peculiar about him, something individual. I found out at last what it was: it was his eyes – beautiful large blue eyes which, if I may put it so, he did not like showing. There was a curious shy look in them, and they seemed quite out of place in that countenance.

When I had studied him for a while, I asked him if he recognised me. "Yes," he said, "I've seen you up in Suhmsgate and Gørbitzgate. But I don't know who you are."

I grew hot all over – what a memory! Egil Halle smiled.

"Do you know who you are talking to?" he asked.

"No," said Nazi 1. "I only know that I've seen him in Gørb-

itzgate

and Suhmsgate several times; I never forget a face".

Good God, so we had passed one another and not recognised one another. I was innocent in the eyes of the law; it was not my job to catch informers.

"It's Max Manus," said Egil.

I cannot help laughing when I think of Nazi 1's face. No doubt he saw in his mind's eye how he could have distinguished himself – captured me or at any rate shot me and done his chiefs, Fehmer and Co., a service.

Now he just became oily and greasy and cringed worse than ever. I could have hit him in the face for sheer disgust...

We went on board all ships, kicked the Germans out of the cabins and had them up on deck. Here and there we found "Germans" girls'. Up on deck with them too, and ashore. Clothes or no clothes, we were giving no exceptions. We were looking for Gestapo, but we could take care of Germans' girls as well. We went from cabin to cabin and found everywhere the same creatures in underclothes, all cringing and wagging their tales. The master race in adversity!

The small boats everywhere, and the small barges which lay at Sjursøya were full of butter, bacon and other food. The poor Home Front boys had seen nothing like it for years, and it was painful to have to tell them that they must not supply their wants now. At one place we found many pairs of rubber boots, Norwegian, the Viking trade mark. Everywhere it was the *same; the cargo consisted of Norwegian things which the Germans had stolen.*

Our professional informers went from one German to another and pointed out their friends in the Gestapo. It was revolting. We went round with Nazi 1 in a small boat, and I asked him why he did not try to escape. We should shoot if he did, he said. That might be much the best thing, I suggested; but he said no, he wanted a proper trial and sentence.

Nazi 1 told me later how he had been blown up with the whole house in which he was living. It was the time some boys had tried to do him in. He said that his famous dog had growled, and just as he took hold of his pistol the explosion came. He actually saw the roof go up, and then tum- bled right down into the cellar. He had lain down at the bottom of the ruins for an hour and a half and had heard someone shout that there was no one left alive there. But he had cried out, "yes. I'm here." He was very proud of the way in which he had directed the searchlights till they had found him. He had been lying pinned down under a beam; one arm was completely crushed. "Yes, Nazi 1" I thought, "we're grateful for your help, but you must expect at least some months in the cage."

APPENDIX II

The German occupation of Norway lasted from April 9th 1940 until May 8th 1945. To Max and his comrades the most feared German in the capital of Oslo in those days was undoubtedly Siegfried Wolfgang Fehmer. My mother *Tikken* met him various times since her first husband, my British father, had been taken prisoner by the Germans. As a British diplomat, he would later be exchanged with a German and sent to neutral Sweden.

Also my uncle, the politician and bank manager Sjur Lindebrække, met Fehmer. and both my mother and her brother have left testimonies of his great personal charm and charisma.

Here, however, I want to reproduce Max' report stated in his book **Underwater Saboteur:**

Fehmer

Then came the great moment which I have dreamed of and longed for all these years – the meeting with our enemy No.1, the man whom we hated more than any other just because we feared him more than any other. The man whom, in spite of everything and much against our will, we respected for his courage and his hellish efficiency. The man who could charm and deceive woman who came to plead for husband or son, so that they went home reassured and grateful and told their fam-

ily and friends that all would go well, for now they had talked to the chief himself and he was so kind and straightforward. Poor women, poor everyone who came up against this fascinating Gestapo chief - Siegfrid Wolfgang Fehmer.

Never in the history of Norway has a name inspired so much death as that of this detested Fehmer. How often we talked of how delightful it would be to fill him with lead! But the very thought of the reprisals which would follow gave every one of us still more nightmares than we were tormented with before. But now Fehmer was caught, and caught in the stillest way imaginable. Fehmer, the brilliant Gestapo chief who knew all about us, and who had thoroughly studied all our methods, had been caught by two ordinary Milorg boys through his affection for his dog, a large black sheepdog. Typically, German to the last – contempt for human life, devotion to his dog.

I will not go into details about an affair in which I myself was not concerned, but one of the two boys has told me how they got hold of Fehmer, who had disappeared without a trace. They had a person under observation and listened into his telephone for a long time without hearing anything interesting. But then suddenly they picked up an inquiry after 'Schock', and realised at once that this was Fehmer's dog. And then Fehmer's activities in this world began to draw to a close. The boys decided that the inquiry must have something to do with Fehmer. A trap was laid, and a German hospital nurse walked straight into it. She admitted that she was an emissary for a man, the contacts were revealed and ended at an Obergefriter (corporal) in a German camp. And so, in the middle of the night, Fehmer was woken with a pistol in his chest. All he said was that he could not think of how they had found him.

I drove down to Akershus to interrogate him about various things. I was in uniform, and had smartened myself up specially for the meeting. I was more nervous than I had been at any time during the war, without being able to explain why.

Then the warders opened the door, and I stepped in. I told them be- forehand that I wanted to be with him alone. And there stood Fehmer, rigidly at attention. He had only trousers on. I looked at him, and he said politely in English: "I am sorry that I am not properly dressed."

"That doesn't matter," I said, "You can talk Norwegian." (Fehmer spoke Norwegian admirably.)

He stood waiting for me to speak. The cell was small, but spotlessly clean. Fehmer spent the day scrubbing and cleaning both himself and the cell and doing gymnastics. He was still very brown and appeared to be in splendid condition. He had a strong supple body.

There was a chair in the cell, and I sat down. Neither of us spoke;

there was complete silence, while the warders outside stood listening eagerly – a strange, gruesome situation. I coughed, and at last found my tongue.

"Do you recognise me?"

"No-o". He hesitated slightly. "I don't" he said at last rather slowly. "My name is Manus."

"Are you Max Manus? What fun! May I congratulate you? You have much to be proud of."

He's a diplomat to the last, I thought, as I gave him a cigarette. And then he told me all I wanted to know.

We sat together in the cell, but we had exchanged roles. I ought to have hated him, I wanted to hate him, but I could not have done him an injury to save my life. The picture I had painted in my imagination faded out completely. What need was there for vengeance when his punishment was complete? I could strike him, I could spit on him, I could inflict the deepest humiliation on him with words, but what for? He had been rendered harmless, what more could I ask?

I plied him with cigarettes, and we talked of my escape from Ullevål hospital, of Gregers and Tallak, of Olav and Roy, and our sabotage jobs. Fehmer smoked greedily. He told me that he had thought he had me tree times, but I had got away, he did not know how. He knew everything that was worth knowing about us. I asked why he never managed to catch us at a control post. He knew that we drove cars, he knew that 28 and 24 were buzzing about the town all day, always in petrol-driven cars.

"Oh," said Fehmer, "it was so hard to spare competent men for control work.

The time passed, and we worked our way nearer and nearer to the sabotage of Donau. And now Fehmer really woke up, his eyes shone and I felt that he had forgotten where he was. He was talking as an expert now, sunning himself in his own efficiency. Yes, yes, of course he knew it was I who had been on the job. As soon as he had been up in that flat at Bygdø Allé 117 and found the limpets and propaganda, he had said "Max Manus." The Donau job had been done well, jawohl. But it would not have worked the next time. He knew we should come back and have another try. He had made thorough investigations and had found the rubber suits under the jetty. Then he had understood at once what had happened. Would it amuse me to hear what he had thought of doing as a counter-move? He was going to stretch thin wires under the jetty, and these would be connected up with an alarm system. He would drench the whole area under the jetty with gas as soon as we came near the wires. He was going to place searchlights and machine-guns. No indeed, we should not have had a chance. He had thought out the whole thing personally... But then the war came to an end.

Fehmer came back to reality – the bare little room, the chair, the table, the iron gratings. I had no desire for vengeance; he was a fallen enemy, even when he stood there glowing with professional pride. He had forgotten the ice baths, forgotten the tortures, forgotten all the evil memories. He had said his piece, and now it was my turn. I did what I think was worse for him than being kicked: I tried to hurt his vanity. I told him that he had fallen into a carefully laid trap. It was just to deceive him that we had laid the rubber suits under the jetty, to divert attention from the hole under the lift. (The suits were those which we had left behind after the Monte Rosa job). And then I explained to him how we had got the Donau. He did not say a word during the whole explanation, but merely followed with interest. I thought I could see his brain work on new plans, new attacks and new counter-moves, and felt how intensely he was still living in a world which no longer existed.

Then I rose silently and went out of the cell.

Nazi 2, the informer, sat in the cell beyond, but I will not speak of my meeting with him. The bare mention of his name gives me a nasty taste in my mouth.

Outside the walls I inhaled the fresh air. The sun shone, the sky was blue, I was a free man and could go where I liked. Behind me in the cells sat my enemies. Every minute, day and night, they awaited the inevitable. The times they may have longed for the merciful words of command which would free them from their nightmares and their vision of shrieking victims whom they had tortured to death when they were the master race or its minions...